CHOICE CUTS
STORIES

CHOICE CUTS

STORIES

JOE CLIFFORD

For my lovely wife, Justine

TABLE OF CONTENTS

UNPUBLISHED MANUSCRIPT #36

Kitty peeled dead flies off the screen. She squinted in the direction of the boatyard. "No boats today," she muttered to herself.

A late season heat wave had brought a constant haze that made it hard to see out over the bay.

A few feet behind her, Jimmy lay on the skinny bed, hands behind his head, eyes transfixed on the tiny television. He was watching a program about botflies on PBS. The sound was turned down low, but he could still hear it, could still see the victims, their arms red and inflamed from infection, the after-effect of larva gestating and hatching under the skin.

Kitty turned from the door and sat at the small round motel table. She picked up a book of matches and began lighting them, one after the other, burning each down to her fingers before letting them drop.

On the first floor below, excited kids raced along the boardwalk, anxious to beat their parents to the beach.

Kitty tried to appear preoccupied by the little fires in her hand, until all the matches were burned out.

"I spoke with my folks the other day," she said. "I don't know what you expect me to tell them. I mean, what *do* you want me to tell them? What is it again you say you do for a living?" Kitty examined her fingernails, crossed and then uncrossed her legs. She bit off a piece of dead skin from her fingertips. "Oh, that's right, you're *a writer*. Y'know, Jimmy, I am pretty sure to be a writer you actually have to *write* once in a while. I mean, I know you don't think I'm very smart, but I *do* know that."

"*At first, the painful bite is indistinguishable from a common bee sting or horsefly bite.*"

"But then again, Jimmy, you don't really *do* anything, do you? You don't even have a drinking problem. Aren't all writers supposed to have drinking problems?"

"The egg deposited, the botfly uses pointed mouth hooks to bore deep down through the skin."

Ever since he was a kid, Jimmy had been terrified of parasites. He found the very small in this life much more unsettling than the very big.

When Jimmy left college to try to make it on his own as a writer, he found that money runs out fast. And because he wouldn't work (citing the severe time constraint a day job would place upon his art) eventually he was forced to take shelter down at the bowery. There, he met a guy with scabies. It wasn't the empty stomach; it wasn't the squalor alone. It wasn't the slew of rejection letters that made him quit that first time. It was the scabies that made him move back home.

"Hey, Jimmy, didn't Hemingway have a drinking problem? I mean, I know I didn't go to college or nothin', but I know Hemingway drank a lot."

Doing heavy damage to muscle tissue, the larva feeds off its immobilized host."

"And who's that other guy you like so much? What's his name, the faggot? The one that wrote that movie? I know *he* had a drinking problem."

The far-off grind of trucks making a final downshift before speeding up to get on the freeway blew in with salt-flavored winds from the beach; it came through the screen door, the heart-breaking sound of diesel engines and seagulls.

Kitty scratched her head, tugged at her dirty sun-bleached hair and stood up. She straightened the towel she had wrapped around her waist and, peering over her shoulder, lifted up the back of it, swatting off any dust that might be on her backside.

"I'm going down the beach," she said, no longer sounding annoyed. She snatched her little square purse off the television, knocking the oversized motel key to the floor.

At the sink in the back of the room, Kitty grabbed a wicker bag from the open closet. The bright lights unflattering, she didn't bother with the mirror. She threw some belongings into her bag and walked out the door.

Jimmy didn't look up, not even when the screen door slammed or when he heard the squeal of brakes. He didn't look up when an ice cream truck passed by or when a girl shouted something in the distance about a "no-talent impotent fuck," as she walked along the boardwalk, on her way to the beach.

Jimmy was mesmerized by the botflies. He wondered how such a tiny bug could bring about so much devastation.

RAGS TO RICHES

Viola Bramble. That's where this starts. With that bitch and a bum named Lucky.

I've been told to begin by explaining who I am. Like anybody with a TV set doesn't know who Harley Tate is. Only the guy behind *Next Big Thing*, *The Candyman Can*, and *Fright Zone*. And if you haven't heard of those, all of which pushed the boundaries of reality TV where few dared to go, you've been living under a rock larger than what they're slinging in South Central these days. Who's Harley Tate? Only a goddamn pioneer at the forefront of reality television programming for the better part of a decade, that's who.

But I'm not here to dwell on my work history, however impressive. I'm here to give my full written confession. Because without it, the prosecution says there can be no deal. No deal, and the next show Harley Tate produces will be from behind bars at Chino State Prison.

So let's start with The Show.

Rags to Riches. The cultural phenomenon that re-defined reality TV, and what ultimately brought me here.

You certainly know the premise by now, since *Rags* is responsible for effectively ending *Survivor*'s tyrannous reign at the top. The premise, simple, brilliant, and all mine: Ten homeless contestants compete for a chance at a new life, a house in Dreamy Vista Villas and one million dollar cash prize.

Pretty sweet deal, eh?

You'd think so. But when the touchy-feely press got wind, it was open season on yours truly. You might recall the editorials, like the one they printed in that advocacy rag the *LA Weekly*, about how "hopelessness had met morally bereft," calling my show "a new way to fail humanity." Before a single episode aired, the normally bipartisan *TV Guide* equated *Rags to Riches* with "YouTube bumfighting for the masses." Ouch.

Then shocked, appalled, and repulsed America helped R2R earn a remarkable 45.3% share in its debut, more than most fucking Super Bowls.

Still, naysayers bashed even the most innocuous challenges, however ultimately rewarding, like when our ten contestants had to go twenty-four hours without a drink to win a new pair of shoes. Here we are stopping these boozers from killing themselves with poison, and *one* guy gets the delirium tremens and needs to be hospitalized, and watch the hands wring. No one was pointing out the good we were doing, how these hobos who defecated in bushes were now getting free medial care, fed and housed. You can guess what happened three episodes later when one of the bums *chose* to eat a fried rat to earn immunity with the Tramp Tribunal.

The network constantly threatened to pull the plug. Which I knew was an empty threat. We were number one in the coveted 18 - 34 year-old demographic, and advertisers were crawling over one another for a thirty-second spot.

Unless you were in a coma, you know what happened at the end of that first season: "Peppermint" Pumpkiss. Bobby "Baggy" Bones. The Kitten Race Trifecta. We drew a 60 share that night. 60!! When corporate called the next day requesting a sit-down, I was expecting a pat on the back, maybe even a much deserved bonus. What I got instead was an order to tone it down. Or else. For Season Two, I would have a partner.

* * *

People like Viola Bramble made me sick. While my youth was abandoned to the flophouses of the bowery so my mother could blow sailors in Echo Park for a nickel bag, Viola was attending finishing school and picking out place settings for her coming out party.

Despite her pedigree, Ms. Bramble wasn't content island hopping in the Galapagos and ball-fisting caviar; no, her life's mission was to make the world a better place. And she wasn't content sparring a few dolphins from the tuna net.

Viola and I got into some pretty heated exchanges early on. Her tree-hugging agenda wanted the "acquisition of life skills" to be the focus of the show, damn the entertainment value. I argued that the focus should be the one million fucking dollars we were giving away. But the brass, forever desperate for positive PR, always took her side.

The highly anticipated kick-off for Season Two had our new crop picking out secondhand suits at the Salvation Army and going through mock interviews in search of gainful employment. The second episode saw the bums learning how to compost and maintain a rooftop garden using reclaimed water. The third, harnessing solar power and the joys of volunteering at a co-op.

Which played out as boring as it sounds.

The only thing keeping us afloat was that America had fallen in love with one of the new contestants, a loveable little scamp who went by the name of Lucky.

You've seen those stupid T-shirts, the ones with the toothless bastard giving the thumbs up, with that fucking motto of his. "Smiles are free!" It was *every*where that fall, couldn't escape it. Worse than "What you talkin' about, Willis?" and "Where's the beef?" combined. When we signed the guy he was living in an abandoned freezer out by the interstate. What the hell did he have to be so happy about?

I didn't like him the minute I met him during our open casting call the preceding summer. Transients from LA's tent city and beyond had lined up around the block. So many people came out, we had to hold the auditions in the parking lot. Festering in the valley heat, the place stank like overripe foot fungus.

The little runt couldn't have stood more than 5'3", a buck thirty, tops. Lucky kept boasting how he'd been "on the wagon" for almost thirty years. Didn't drink? How the hell does somebody live in an abandoned freezer and *not* drink?

The producers fell in love with him instantly.

Lucky had to be pushing sixty, although we never learned his actual age because he had no identification (which made getting a W-2 a bitch, trust me). After he was cast, he frequently tried to saddle up to me, chipper and friendly, like we were going to be best buddies, making small talk and offering pointless observations. He smelled like bum shit.

But that didn't stop him from getting all chummy with the rest of the staff, the lighting guys, set designers, key grips, all of whom seemed completely taken with his upbeat shtick. Especially Viola.

* * *

The second season was in full swing, Viola and I alone in the screening room. It was very late. We'd been spending more and more nights like this, just the two of us, bouncing ideas, brainstorming, talking into to the midnight hour, the studio closed up and quiet, all the contestants asleep peacefully in their bungalows.

I hated to admit it, but I'd found myself hating her less. For one, it's hard to stay agro at something so damn good looking. Plus, once you got past the granola politics, the girl had something— an edge, a spark, a little sassiness that made her almost fun to be around.

"Are you going to give me *any* credit, Harley?" she asked, fingering through remnants of the day's fruit and cheese plate, before settling on a plump fig, which she wrapped her full lips around and set upon sucking like a chubby thumb.

"Credit? For what?" I struck a match and lit a cigarette. "Being a pain in my ass?"

"Ratings are up."

"Ratings are up because *you* brought them down in the first place."

"Oh, Harley," she said with a sly grin. "You're such a curmudgeon."

"I'm younger than you are, Viola."

She sat on the buffet table, long legs dangling, skirt showing a lot of toned and tanned skin, white blouse unbuttoned one below casual.

I crossed the floor, slipped off my sport's jacket, and leaned against the table with her.

"Why are you so angry?" she asked.

I craned behind her, found a corn chip still intact and dug around a giant bowl of what used to be guacamole.

"Really, Harley, from where I sit, I see a sharp, successful, good looking guy—"

I caught her eye. "Good looking?"

Viola slapped my arm. "I mean it. Ever since I met you, you walk around here, skulking, like you're pissed off at the world. What the hell happened to you as a child?"

"You want to know what happened?"

"Relax, it's a figure of speech."

"No, I'll tell you. My old man was a drunken fuck who split before I was born. My mother, a dope fiend, would disappear for days in the bowels of the million dollar hotels of Spring Street, consorting with the merchant marines on layover looking for a good time, if you know what I mean. My earliest memories are of sailors taking me for long walks on the pier. Before she protracted the virus and dropped dead, we lived on welfare and food stamps, which my mother usually sold to the Mexican down the street for a hit."

"Jesus, I'm sorry." She sat upright, all playfulness gone from her face. "I was just teasing. I didn't mean to—"

"What? Bring up reality? Hey, baby, that's life. Reality's a bitch."

Viola reached for my hand, taking it in hers. "You should be proud of yourself, for pulling yourself out of that, for not ending up a—"

"A what? A Bum?" I sneered. "Goddamn right."

"You really hate these people, don't you?"

"I don't hate anybody. But I sure as hell don't pity them either. Why should I? They're losers, getting wasted on drugs and alcohol so they don't have to deal with the consequences of their shitty choices. And why should they? The state will always send them a check."

"Or they can come on your show," she said, sadly.

"Fucking-A right."

I was really stewing when she did it—leaned over and kissed me on the cheek. Startled the hell out of me.

There was a loud knock on the door and Viola jumped to her feet, straightening her skirt. The door pushed open.

"Hope I ain't disturbin' nothin'?" Lucky said with an aw-shucks smile, showcasing the new dental bridge we'd provided. "Got some ideas 'bout the show wanna run by ya!"

The contestant bungalows were way over in the studio's northwest corner, past props and wardrobe, which meant the little bastard just walked damn near three-quarters a mile to offer an opinion about *my* show, like I gave a shit what a man like him thought.

I collected my notes by the plasma, and tried to catch Viola's eye on the way out but she was already buying whatever Lucky was selling.

Back at my place in Malibu, I couldn't sleep and spent most of the night tossing and turning. On my way into work the next day, I bought some flowers from a Mexican at a roadside stand, but when I realized how stupid it was, I threw them out on the Pacific Coast Highway.

* * *

One of the problems with R2R was that as the season wore on the hobos would invariably start to look better. A few weeks with regular meals and access to hot water works wonders. Lesions and abscesses started to heal, color returned to cheeks, pounds put back on.

And no one benefited from these changes more than Lucky. You'd see him walking around the lot with newfound confidence, a spring in his step, face fuller and shaven, hair washed, combed, clothes clean like a regular person.

We still had a show to put on, though. This was my favorite part of the day, watching the carriage turn back into a rotten pumpkin. The make-up department would whiten Lucky's skin to its natural grayish hue, reapplying the dark circles, repainting the sores and abscesses.

Best of all was when they'd remove the dental bridge.

Sometimes Lucky would catch me watching his humiliation, and I could see that he wanted to smile but was too ashamed. I guess smiles aren't so "free" after all.

After that night when we got hot and heavy in the screening room, Viola seemed to be avoiding me. I wasn't being overly sensitive, either. I could seldom catch her alone, our conversations clipped, and she all but stopped contributing ideas for the show. Fine by me. She still hung around the set, but mostly to fraternize with the riff-raff, especially Lucky. I didn't know what game she was playing, but I didn't give a damn. Freed from Viola's interference, I was doing some of my best work.

We shot the penultimate episode of Season Two at the produce markets downtown using hidden cameras, the challenge being to see which bum could steal the most fruit. You know what happens to a vagrant trying to steal produce from a sidewalk vendor in LA? Middle Easterners receive less of a thrashing for swiping a falafel! I'd stipulated that no one step in until after the police arrived.

Lucky won immunity, propelling him into the finale.

* * *

It was the night before the last episode of the season. Lucky was to square off against Steamboat Willie, an African-American ox who used to bare-knuckle brawl during the Nixon Administration, in a live broadcast, a first for the program. The whole nation would be watching.

The evening air was brisk, much colder than usual. I'd hung around the set until most were gone for the day, chain-smoking, trying to think of ways to tip the scale in Steamboat's favor. An exiting staffer said Viola was in her trailer and that she wanted to see me. It was the first I'd heard from her all day.

I crossed the dark parking lot. A chill desert wind whisked through the valley.

If she thought she could spring a bunch of last-minute changes on me, she was sorely mistaken.

The curtains were parted enough for me to see Viola sitting on the sofa, oversized T-shirt and shorts, hair tousled, like she'd just finished canoeing on a camping trip. I felt like a voyeur, but I was too transfixed to move. She looked beautiful.

Then he walked out of the can. The pipsqueak had just come out of the shower, towel wrapped around his waist, pigeon chest showcasing sailor tattoos, dripping wet.

Lucky smiled big, flashing that new dental bridge.

I wanted to throw up.

* * *

The first television show I worked on out of college was a criminal investigation program, and I remember overhearing the writers talk about what drives a killer to murder, how they're overcome with rage or blinded by jealousy and don't know what they're doing, and I always thought it was bullshit, just another way for the criminal to escape justice. But later that evening, after I'd silently backed away from her window and headed out to my car, making sure to drive slowly past the night watchman on my way out, after I'd driven the mile and a half from the set, parking on the desolate dirt road that led into the ravine, returning on foot submerged in the shadows while the rest of the world stood still—after I scaled the fence in the remote northwest corner of the lot with the can of gasoline, creeping toward the small, one-man efficiencies on the back edge of the property where Lucky now slept, I can't say for sure it was me doing those things. And I can't say it wasn't. It was more like a television viewer so entranced by his favorite program that he had become part of the show.

I watched the killer douse the wood, strike the match, step back and watch it burn bright, wild orange flames dancing in the cool valley night, the shot fading to black.

Of course, I'd known about Steamboat Willie's criminal record; background checks were a part of the casting process. Although the breaking and entering charges had been a decade old, I also knew that as far as motives go, a million dollar prize is a pretty good one. Steamboat must've known it too, because he accepted a manslaughter plea almost immediately.

As for the show, as you know, we didn't have that finale, but that didn't exactly hurt the hype. The murder landed us on the cover of *Newsweek* and *People*, set us up with Oprah, Tyra, Ellen, and everywhere in between. Best of all, Lucky's death had turned me into a martyr, lauded by the same press that had once vilified me, as I choked back tears for "America's loss of a true inspiration."

R2R was put on hiatus, but I knew it wouldn't last. The scandal and its fallout conspired to create a fevered pitch. How I was looking forward to that third season! Who wouldn't be tuning in for *that*?

Viola had removed herself from her advisory role, and good riddance. She never even said goodbye. And I was glad. How could I look her in the eye after what I'd seen?

Eventually the network couldn't deny the dollar signs, and I was told to start up again. *Rags to Riches* was back! And ol' Harley was sure to get a few guarantees in writing this time.

* * *

Saturday morning, I'd been unable to sleep. So many ideas swirling around my head, I'd gotten an early start. I was envisioning a *Rags to Riches' Road Race*, as homeless contestants all across America set out on a scavenger hunt. I saw motorized shopping carts and tricked-out mobile homes, rogue Greyhound buses soaring like black swans through hobo jungles. It would be awesome.

Sitting in my Malibu study, fresh latte by my keyboard, I'd just finished banging out some killer script ideas when the phone rang. Viola. Asking if she could come over.

We stood on my back patio, overlooking the canyon that separated my spread from Mark Burnett's house, a monstrosity. The sun blazed through valley smog, evaporating the morning dew from the foliage. I leaned over the rails, relishing how uncomfortable Viola was; I could literally feel her squirming in her guilt. The deck extended out over the canyon and its three hundred foot drop to the dry brush and rock below. I loved the view from my deck, especially in the morning.

"I'm sorry I never said goodbye, Harley."

I shrugged and lit a cigarette.

"I'm sure you saw how close Lucky and I had become."

"Of course," I said. "His death got to us all." It looked like Mark was constructing a new addition. Like the eyesore wasn't big enough. Insecure prick.

"We became *very* close."

"I know. Tough loss. For all of us." I turned to face her. " You'll forgive me for being blunt, but if you're looking to get back in, I'm afraid that ship has sailed. *Rags* is all mine. I have it in writing from the network."

"I don't care about the show."

"Good." I walked toward the sliding glass doors. "Then if you'll excuse me—"

Viola didn't move. I didn't like the look on her face. She reached into her purse and extracted a picture, passing it along.

It was an old tattered photograph, black and white, fading to yellow. A diminutive man was smiling with his arm around a small boy at the end of a pier. The boy couldn't have been more than five. The man had sailor tattoos. The boy held an ice cream cone. Seagulls flapped in the summer sky. I started to sweat.

"Turn it over," she said.

On the back, a date from long ago, and a couple scribbled names, the last same as mine. His real name had been Stephen.

"It's why we called you to the trailer that night. He'd finally gotten up the courage to tell you. He'd been so nervous, he hadn't showered or eaten for days." She grabbed my arm, eyes welling. "I've struggled these past few months over what to do."

I turned the photograph back over, studied the faces again, seeing each in the other.

Viola moved closer. "He was the one who asked me to let you do the show the way you wanted. It made him happy to see you happy. He was backing out of the competition. He didn't care about the money. He'd only signed up to get closer to you."

The photograph. I remembered that day vividly, waves crashing beneath the dock, the gulls squawking overhead, how safe I'd felt.

"I know how much you hated your father, but if you knew the whole story, Harley. He spent his whole life looking for you, but your mother moved you around, kept you two apart. You know that's why he got sober? He stayed sober all those years just on the chance he'd find you some day."

I shielded my eyes from the valley's blistering sun.

"I guess you were right," Viola said as tears rolled down her cheeks. "Reality is a bitch."

FAVORS

When my father was getting ready to die last year, he made me promise to look after Madeline, his new wife. At the time it seemed like a simple promise. They'd met over canasta at the Sunny Gates trailer park down in Sunnyvale, six months before he was diagnosed with brain cancer. Although I hadn't gotten the chance to know her that well, Madeline seemed pleasant enough, even if she wasn't exactly Dad's type.

After Dad finally retired, he could've gone anywhere he wanted but he picked Sunny Gates. I guess I could see the appeal. These weren't low rent shacks but upscale trailers on finely groomed lots in a seniors' community, with around the clock staff and care. They even had a little market on the grounds that delivered groceries.

My father had been a tremendous success, and growing up I hoped to be just like him. The year he made partner in the law firm, my mother died. Still, he raised his only son and kept his affairs in order, continuing to litigate some of the Bay Area's biggest civil liberty cases. I attended the Top of the Mark ceremony when he received his Lifetime Achievement Award for his work with the Bridges and Hands Foundation, a nonprofit group that provides services to teenage runaways. I swelled with pride.

After he passed, I made arrangements with Madeline to take her to breakfast one Sunday a month. At first, the trips were painless. I'd get up early and on my way through Marin stop for a cappuccino and hummus wrap—because Madeline always insisted on going to Denny's, a restaurant where I refused to eat.

It was during one of these visits that I first heard about her son, Winky.

I didn't know Madeline even had a son. I couldn't recall Dad's ever mentioning him. As details about Winky's life began to emerge, I understood why. I caught a few references about his "having gone away" at one time, something I assumed to mean prison, although I never asked for clarification, and Madeline never offered any.

It is one thing to agree to do favors for somebody; it is quite another doing favors for the person who *is* the favor. Which is what started to happen. Small things at first. Madeline would ask me to drop off clothes to Winky. Once it was a DVD player, another time an envelope with a twenty-dollar bill in it. Before long, Winky needed a ride on Wednesday or Friday because his car had broken down. Winky lived in the city, which has more than adequate public transportation. But Winky needed a ride, nevertheless. I later discovered that he didn't even own a car.

I was often tempted to refuse these requests, as I felt my generosity being taken advantage of, but I'd made a promise to Dad and wanted to believe I'd inherited his sense of philanthropy.

Winky lived in the Mission, which has its good and bad spots. Winky's place was somewhere in-between. From the outside, his apartment on 30th and San Jose wasn't exactly the skids, but it wasn't high class either.

During these initial encounters, I kept conversation to a minimum and Winky didn't appear the talkative type. Still, I was never entirely comfortable around him. A wiry fellow who seemed perpetually distracted, he was too tall and skinny, always dressed in some angry graphic tee and dirty jeans. I had my suspicions he was on drugs, but what a man wants to do in the privacy of his own home is none of my business. Best I could muster about his employment status was that Winky didn't have any. Once I took him to the Social Security office, so I thought he might be on some kind of disability, but he didn't seem particularly addled, and it didn't make any difference to me.

* * *

The last Sunday of October, Madeline and I were at Denny's on South Mathilda. As usual, I'd offered to take her somewhere better, but she said she liked their biscuits. There was no point asking. Madeline didn't strike me at the sort who could appreciate good cuisine anyway.

This morning, she ate dreadfully slow, pawing at dry biscuits with clumsy fingers, crumbs spraying everywhere. I drank the swill they tried passing off as coffee.

"I think Winky's in trouble," Madeline said, her mouth full of plum lipstick and dough.

I flagged down a waitress. "The check?"

"Would you be a dear and make sure he's all right?"

I reached for my wallet. "I'd love to help, but I can't today," I said, extracting a ten. "I have to drive to Sacramento and pick up briefs. I'm in court tomorrow."

The waitress, a middle-aged cuss with fried red hair, slapped the check on the table like she'd been inconvenienced to do her job.

Madeline sighed. "It's so hard being a mother. You never stop wanting what's best for your children."

It was an obvious ploy. My father's desire to help the lower classes notwithstanding, I couldn't help but speculate how lonely Dad must've been to marry into this family. Her eyes began to well.

"OK," I said, biting. "What makes you think Winky's in trouble?"

She placed a crust carefully on her plate. "He called the other day from the bus station. He was talking about the strangest things, how people were after him, and if he never saw me again... I wouldn't ask, but I'm worried. He's my boy. And I'm sure your father—"

All right, I said. I'd drop by on my way through the city.

By the time I made it back to the Bay, the fog had rolled in. Exiting on Cesar Chavez, I found the entire district infested, lamp-posts, traffic signs, produce markets, all swallowed up in dense pockets of wet gray.

Far as I knew, Winky didn't have a phone, but he always seemed to be expecting me. Usually he'd come downstairs right away and take whatever trinket I was passing off, so I never had to see the inside of his second floor apartment. This time when I rang the bell, he hollered for me to come up. I would've rather we stuck with our usual routine.

Heading through the unlocked gate, I felt the murkiness trail me inside.

All of Winky's lights were off, and there weren't any shades on the windows, a soft gray filling the room.

Even though it was close to noon, Winky looked like he'd just woken up. He didn't have a shirt on, only the same pair of dirty jeans he always wore, not even buttoned all the way up. I noticed the tattoos on his shoulders and flanks, all with shaky black outlines. Naked girls and barbed wired phrases like, "In Loving Memory" and "Never Forget," whatever the hell that meant. He looked scruffier than usual.

He told me to have a seat and asked if I wanted some coffee. I like to be polite regardless of the company, so I accepted. The coffee, that is. The only place to "sit" was a couch I had no intention of going near—foam bursting at the seams, strange blotchy stains—who knew the parasites breeding in there. Water burbled through old clanking pipes. The place stank of gas leaks and animal fur; and I didn't see any pets.

Winky went into the kitchen, and I listened to cupboard doors open and shut, a kettle fill under the faucet.

I looked around. Crap everywhere. Pop cans sawed in half and spent matchbooks. A tiny TV with foiled rabbit ears sat atop a milk crate, the type of TV they don't make anymore. The corner to a big blue blanket, which I assumed functioned as a window shade, was tacked to a frame and draped to the floor. The walls were riddled with yawning holes, exposing plaster and the wood planks behind it. What sort of person chooses to live like this?

"Winky," I said, "I just saw your mother—"

"Oh, yeah," he said, poking his head out. "Today's Sunday, ain't it? How she doin'?"

"She's fine."

"Went to breakfast?"

"Yes, I took her to breakfast. It was a lovely meal. Listen, she asked me to stop by. She's worried about you. Said she thought you might be in some... trouble."

I heard the toilet flush and a door slam, and a girl emerged from the blackness of the hallway. She couldn't have been more than fifteen. Walking toward me in a crooked line, she wore a teeny denim skirt all twisted up, wife-beater tee, with black bra straps showing underneath and falling off the shoulder. Waif-thin with bleached-out hair, she frantically scratched her arm inside the elbow. When she passed, she didn't look up. I caught the ripe odor of sex and overly fruity perfume. She plopped on the couch and fidgeted with her legs.

Winky didn't bother to introduce us, and I began to grow indignant. It's one thing for a man like Winky to choose that lifestyle; it is quite another for a girl that age.

With his arms stretched inside the kitchen doorframe, bony body elasticized, he began swinging back and forth slowly, a perverted monkey. I studied his face. There was something in his eyes I hadn't noticed before, a desperate, dangerous quality. They were sunken and yellow and mean.

"So Moms sent baby brother to check up on me," he said.

Police sirens whirred by the windows, flashing blues and reds.

"I mean, your dad married my mom, right?"

"And what's your point?" I said.

"No point, Sporto. Just that would make us brothers is all." He looked past me. I didn't like the way he did it either, all wolfish.

I couldn't say for sure if he and the girl were lovers, but the way she laid there, like a limp rag doll, him licking his chops, it was nauseating.

"Hey, Valerie," Winky said. "You know I got a baby brother?"

Valerie flopped on her side. I winced a smile at her. She didn't return the favor.

The kettle whistle blew, and he dropped from the door.

Just leave, I thought. Contact the authorities and be done with it, screw this idiot. But she was so young, helpless; it didn't seem right abandoning her.

"Sorry, bro, don't got no sugar," he said, striding into the room, almost thrusting the hot coffee in my hands.

I didn't know from where this hostility stemmed, if it was for Valerie's benefit or what, but such aggression was seriously misplaced. I hadn't done anything but favors for the guy since we met.

"Why don't you sit down, Sporto?" Winky shrugged his shoulders, as if offended. Then he affected a dreadful southern accent. "Val, I don't think baby brother likes our home."

I had no interest in playing this game. I held up my hands. "Your mom asked me to stop by and make sure you're OK. You say you are, good enough for me. I didn't mean any disrespect."

"Sure, Sporto," he said, his voice trailing to a whisper. Then his whole demeanor changed in a sudden effort to feign humility.

"Actually, there is something you could do for me—me and Val, I mean."

"What?" I said.

"No biggie. Just a ride. Not far. Half an hour, tops." He plucked his cigarettes from his jeans and lighted one from the burner.

"Hey," Valerie said, finally speaking up. "Gimme that." Her voice was high and small.

He flicked the lit cigarette over my head and it landed on her belly. She flinched with a delayed reaction, then picked up the burning cigarette and sleepily swatted away the ash.

"I mean, if you think you can hang," Winky said. "I know Moms would appreciate it." He winked. "I could pay you, if you like." He patted down his pockets, like he had money, and like I'd take it if he did.

* * *

"Nice ride, Sporto."

"You've been in my car before, Winky."

"True, but Val hasn't, and I ain't never told you how much I like Bentleys."

"It belonged to my father," I said.

They were piled in the back. He slouched, reclining with one leg up, she wedged in-between. He had his arm around her neck, holding her there, letting his fingers roam and molest, trying to act nonchalant when he made a push for between her legs. Once she and I caught eyes in the rearview, but I couldn't read a thing; she seemed so disaffected.

Winky said he had to go down to Daly City "to see a friend." I wasn't naïve. I spent a lot of time in the city and wasn't as sheltered as I may've looked. I'd read Baudelaire and Bukowski, seen *Mean Streets* and *Taxi Driver*. I knew plenty about the darker side of life.

"I'm not doing anything illegal," I said, "so you can forget that right now."

"*Illegal*? You hear that?" he said, pretending to ask Valerie for her opinion. "You've read too many books there, Sporto. Do I look like the kind of guy that'd do something illegal?" He spat out a low laugh.

I wasn't worried. He looked the part, not me. More importantly, I wanted the chance to talk to this girl, find out where her parents were, why she stayed with this creep. I felt as though the fates had delivered me there, and I could only hope that whatever business he had, he'd be tending to it alone.

I cut across Precita St., the fog thicker still, entering the freeway and taking the 280 split south as a light rain began to fall. Winding down the valley, there was no traffic; no one spoke in the car, leaving only the sounds of slow breathing and wet tires on asphalt.

In Daly City, we pulled into an apartment complex, a half dozen tenements spaced out. Winky directed me to pull into a parking garage, guiding me down to the bottom level and a far corner with no other cars. I cut the engine.

Winky whispered something in Valerie's ear as he was getting out, and told me he'd be right back. Then he opened a cellar door and disappeared into the darkness, and I was left alone with her.

Where to begin?

The world's a screwed up place, I know. But most people in bad spots are clowns like Winky, adults who make bad decision after bad decision; they get what they deserve. What about Valerie? Despite the way she dressed or whatever she'd allowed herself to become, she was still just a kid. I knew one thing: my father wouldn't turn his back.

"How long have you known Winky?" I asked, by way of ice-breaker.

"I dunno," she mumbled, chewing the side of her thumb and staring out the window.

How do you ask the questions I wanted to ask? Why aren't you cheerleading and having sleepovers, popping popcorn and giggling about boys instead of defiling your body with a slimball old enough to be your father?

In the mirror, her lax, suggestive positioning left nothing to the imagination, and I felt my face flush.

"How long have you lived in the city, Valerie?"

"You got any gum?"

"Yeah, I think so." Happy to be doing something for her, I opened the middle console, sifting through my receipts and day planner until I found a pack.

When I sat back up, she was poised directly behind my seat. Animated as hell, bouncy, like an overly stimulated kitten. She snatched the chewing gum from my hand and giggled.

"You like me?" she asked.

"Sure. I mean, I just met you, but yes, I like you."

"I like you, too." She leaned over and gave me a peck on the cheek, then slithered between the leather seats up front. Facing me, resting on her haunches, she nibbled on her lip and eased herself forward, hand creeping over my lap. I grabbed her wrist and she squealed in delight.

I pulled her close. I wanted to tell her that she misunderstood me, that I was there to help her. But it all happened so fast, and honorable intentions got twisted into something perverted, wrong. Valerie moved her mouth to my ear, her breath hot. She whispered to let her go, and I let her go. Her head sank between my thighs and I closed my eyes.

* * *

Valerie sat curled in my lap while I stroked her hair. Of all the thoughts whirling around inside my brain, all the things I wished to tell her, all I said was "What about Winky?" I didn't mean it like that. But that's what came out. What about Winky.

"Winky?" she said with a curious laugh. "He don't care. He said to let you do whatever you wanted."

I pushed her off me, feeling sick and dirty. I stared into her eyes and she stared right back. And I finally understood that look, the one I couldn't quite place back at the apartment and in the rear-view; and it was death and everything cold and hopeless.

She shrugged, then peeled the stick of peppermint chewing gum from its wrapper and popped it into her mouth, gazing wistfully into the darkness. She began snapping little bubbles, lolling her head from side to side. In between snaps, she hummed a soft lullaby in that high, teeny voice of hers, like she didn't have a care in the world.

I fired the ignition. I had no idea where I'd go with her in the car but I needed to get the hell out of there. I'd dump her on the side of the road if need be. My heart was in my throat and I could still taste her sugary sweet strawberry lip gloss all over me. I resisted the urge to retch. I turned to check the side-view and there stood Winky.

He rapped a knuckle and made a winding gesture.

"Turn off the car," he said.

"I'm not turning off anything." I made to shift into reverse.

"How old you think she is, Sporto?"

I looked over at Val, chomping away. She closed her eyes tightly and gave me a big phony grin, jutting her chin forward.

Before I could even think, he whispered in my ear, "She's a lot younger than that. You're a lawyer. You really want the police swabbing that pretty mouth?" He clucked his tongue and patted me on the back. "Might wanna buckle up there, Sporto."

* * *

Winky nudged me down a long stairwell. I felt like I'd been drugged, the world a warped recording playing back in slow motion. The cramped corridor reeked of cleaning chemicals and urine, giant slabs of concrete encasing us, as though in a tomb. We passed a boiler and I could feel its heat raging inside. At the bottom of the well was a door.

Winky pushed it open.

Two big men, arms prison-sculpted, stood off to the side where a kitchen should be, only there was no stove, no refrigerator. Radiator steam hissed. The men didn't look up as they continued measuring out small black lumps on a scale. Above them, a garish painting of Jesus hung, ornate gold frame askew.

Winky put his arm around me, said to relax, that big brother wouldn't let anything bad happen. He led me into the next room where a squat older Mexican stood, hands in pockets, eyes squinty red. It was insufferably hot. Wisps of long gray hair fell from the old Mexican's crown, clinging to his neck and shoulders. He didn't wear a shirt. I stared at the navel of his fat, hairy belly.

The room overflowed with merchandise and electronic goods, TVs, stereos, DVD players, power tools, one stacked on top of the other, the apartment dimly lit by artificial yellow light.

"This him?" the Mexican said to Winky.

The Mexican didn't offer to shake my hand, scowling at me like I was infected. He gestured to a chair in front of him, the only furniture in the room, and ordered me to sit down.

Out the corner of my eye, I spied what at first I thought was a Buddha statue. Then I saw it was a birdbath on its side, cradled in the lap of an elephant god. The Hindus call him Ganesh.

Winky loomed behind my chair and draped his sinewy arms around my neck, letting them dangle down my chest. They were riddled with track marks.

He gestured toward the Mexican. "See, brother, Indio's my partner. We been talking."

The room grew darker, shadows moving in, tiny vibrations traveling across the concrete floor, up my feet and into my wrists. My hands rigidly gripped the armrest.

"Why are you doing this to me?" I asked.

Winky clasped a hand firmly behind my neck. "We don't think what you and your father did was right."

"My father?" I said, trying to turn around. "*My father* spent his life trying to help people like—" He squeezed tighter.

"Gets all up in her, pounding that shit like it's free," Winky said, "and doesn't leave her a dime? Pretty rude, don't you think? We're supposed to be family. Breakfast once a month ain't gonna cut it no more." Winky tsked-tsked. "And what you did upstairs to Val, taking advantage of a little girl like that."

"Winky," I said, pleadingly, "I—I mean, she—"

Winky leaned in, right next to my ear. His breath stank of street vendor stewed pork and pepper. "I wouldn't say nothin' bad about Val, Sporto. That's Indio's niece. You know what we do to sick fucks like you in prison?"

Then the squat, old Mexican's mouth slung open wide, far wider than any human mouth should be allowed to extend, and I felt swallowed whole. And as the walls closed in around me, I knew all the money in the world couldn't buy my way out of this.

THE MEAT

The three men trudged through deep snow that continued to fall, bundled in makeshift rags sewn together, ice matting down heavy beards, the exposed skin around their eyes and mouths burned pink and raw. The food scraps they'd managed to scavenge from meals and steal from the guards' station were gone, so too the vodka that had helped keep them warm and buoy spirits those first few frigid nights. This far north, daylight was clipped to a few precious hours, and as bad was it was now, it would be far worse when night fell. Because that was when the animals came, the wolves and the bears and the Kazakhs hunters who were surely tracking them following news of their escape, each able to strike swiftly, without warning.

"I'm hungry," said Puzanov.

Nikoli lowered his head and fought against the snow and wind.

Puzanov reached for his shoulder, but the fat man moved too slowly to snare him. "We need to eat."

"We will eat," said Leo, wedging in front. "Besides, why should you complain? You've more meat on your bones than both of us combined."

Nikoli glanced over his shoulder, as the corpulent Puzanov dropped his shoulders, huffing like a petulant child.

* * *

Prisoners trying to escape from the labor camp always faced a bleak prospect, which is why the prison had been built where it had, 150 kilometers beneath the Artic Circle, on a small island archipelago, cut off from the mainland and isolated by the inhospitable White Sea. Nikoli had heard rumors of men who had successfully reached the mainland, though he did not put much stock in these campfire stories, any more than he let the prospect of failure deter him. In fact, each time a frozen corpse was hauled back to camp, traded in by the Kazakhs for a sack of tea or wheat, stripped naked and hung on a stake, it only hastened his resolve to be smarter and not end up like the others.

They ascended the rocky summit, holding one another's coattails and stabbing the ground with the walking sticks they'd fashioned from frozen, fallen branches, Puzanov dragging the line like a lead anchor.

Nikoli stared down the long, steep bank and out over the valley, hoping to see shore. Instead he saw nothing but more snow and tall trees sloping downward, an endless sea of white on white peppered with brief moments of deep, dark green.

"We will sleep here," Leo said.

"What about the food?" Puzanov demanded. "We must eat!"

"We *will* eat," said Leo, "but first we must secure shelter. Or we will freeze to death."

"And where will we find this food you promised?" Puzanov said to Nikoli. "This food you told me would come, eh?"

But Nikoli had no answer for him.

A bookseller by trade, Nikoli had had his shop raided by the Bolsheviks late one evening, accused of accepting a bribe from an enemy of the Revolution, meaning he'd sold the wrong book to the wrong man. There had been no eyewitnesses, no trial. It had been six years since he'd last seen his wife and son, six years since any form of communication with them at all. The only pictures that remained were his memories, which became less certain with each passing winter. Whisked away under the dark cover of night, he was corralled with all the others who were expected to die there in the forced labor penitentiary, forgotten without a fight. But Nikoli was a resourceful man, a scholarly man, a man governed by reason and logic. He kept his strength up by stretching, doing pull-ups and push-ups, eating whatever he could find, however slimy or disgusting. He recited passages from the books he could recall to keep his mind sharp, and directed his efforts into finding a way off the island.

It was a simple matter of considering all the variables, eliminating potential pitfalls, not letting emotions get the better him, and following chains of thought to their rationale conclusions. Like knowing when to leave.

Temperatures plummeted well below freezing during the coldest months, but it was a mistake to go during the warmer ones, since warmer currents melted the ice, and those floes would be needed to get to the mainland. Leaving during the coldest months, however, created its own set of obstacles, not the least of which was finding a way to stay warm. And this was not a trip that could be undertaken alone. He would need an ally he could trust, implicitly.

After a careful search and thorough introspection, Nikoli befriended Leo, a doctor, who shared a similar background and came from the same stock. And only when Nikoli was certain he was dealing with a righteous, upstanding man did he unveil his plan. Not that Nikoli had to sell Leo on the idea—every prisoner dreamt escape—it was only a question of how to get away with it. Which Nikoli preached was a rudimentary matter of execution.

Together, the bookseller and doctor had spent countless hours stitching gloves and boots, heavy coats from canvas swathes ripped from potato and rice sacks, threading them with the fine fish bones they used for needles in the converted monastery that served as inmate barracks, biding their time...

Slinking back from the ridge, Nikoli and Leo dropped to their knees beneath a dense eave and began scooping snow for the burrow that would be their bed. The winds swirled up from the ravine, shaking loose more snow from the evergreens and undermining their efforts.

"There is nothing out here," Puzanov said, dismissively waving a hand, as the winds picked up and the sky churned ash and charcoal. "Where will we find food on this wasteland?"

Leo looked to Nikoli.

Nikoli felt his body failing him with each handful. It had been too long without food and the grueling trek was proving too taxing; he knew they would not last much longer.

Reluctantly, Puzanov squatted. "We will die out here without food," he said softly, and began to dig his own hole.

Nikoli and Leo had spent a great deal of time plotting the perfect escape. Though one problem lingered that they could not wrap their collective minds around, no matter how hard they tried: having enough food for the long journey. They could sneak past the guards' station, make it beyond the walls, but there was simply no way to store enough to eat from the camp, and out here, on the barren, cold tundra, hunting was not a realistic option.

It was not without much moral debate that they arrived at their solution, desperate times and desperate measures, the need of two outweighing the need of one: they'd supply their own meat.

The candidate had to be slow-witted, gullible.

Most of all, he had to be fat.

It was Nikoli who struck first, wrapping his arms around Puzanov's beefy neck in a chokehold. The fat man did not immediately react, unable to process what was happening; with wide eyes, he stared out, still a trusting pig unaware he was about to be slaughtered. Leo cracked the empty vodka bottle over his head, and Puzanov squealed and covered up, sinking to his knees. Nikoli and Leo frantically fisted the large shards of broken glass, and began stabbing and slicing wildly through the air, piercing the plump flesh, severing arteries and vessels, puncturing deep organs. The fat man fell forward, face first, dark blood spreading beneath his large, lifeless body, staining the white snow red.

* * *

The growling woke them. The night ink black, without stars or moonlight, and it was snowing harder than before. The racing winds made it hard to hear from which direction the growling came, but it was loud and sounding louder.

Nikoli and Leo scrambled to their feet and tried to run. They did not know where they were running to, or what exactly they were running from. They only knew that they had to get off the mountain. Along the ridge, the ground gave way, a big chunk breaking off like a glacier dropping into the ocean, and Nikoli and Leo fell with it, skidding, sliding, rolling rock over stump, branch over limb, smacking their heads, kidneys, flanks and spines, pulled by gravity, spinning faster and faster, all the way to the bottom.

* * *

Nikoli did not know how long they'd been passed out. The storm had stopped, skies cleared to a light slate grey; only trace flurries remained, aimlessly drifting down. Nikoli's only thought upon waking was of the meat they had left behind.

The men could not climb back up the mountainside. And even if they had been able to, surely the wolves would've gotten what was left by now.

Nikoli scanned ahead and could see the shore. But there were no ice floes to take them to the mainland, only a soft mist that hovered above the water, peaceful and calm.

Perhaps remnants from the storm would carry a floe to the beach. He and Leo must be patient. They must wait. They sat on the pebbled shore.

At first, the men tried to fill the time by talking about their families, how happy they'd be to see them again and restart their lives. They spoke of the farms and the shops and the practices, the wives and the children and the comrades, the better days that were surely coming, but the lack of conviction felled these words like forced prayers in an empty cathedral.

Neither spoke of the meat or what they had done.

Soon they did not speak at all.

Nikoli and Leo sat silently as night returned, the shore and sea receding with regressing light, a yellow crescent moon bobbing in the purple sky. In his pocket, Nikoli thumbed a shard of glass.

He and Leo watched one another, with intense, darting eyes that soon began to wear heavily with fatigue, though it was clear neither dared be the first to fall asleep.

RED PISTACHIOS

The telephone's ringing didn't wake Tom Hazuka. He wasn't asleep. He wasn't awake either. Blackouts are like that.

Head resting on a stack of dreadful portfolios he had yet to grade, he arose slowly, half bottle of rye still gripped in his fist, and kicked through the trash piling up, stumbling into the kitchen.

On the blood-colored stucco wall, the clock read just before midnight. Tom swiped the phone. Too many lights. He dragged a hand down the fixture, sliding his aching body to the floor. The high desert moon shone brightly through the window.

"It's me. Alan. You there?"

"I'm here," Tom said, reaching behind him for the overturned junk drawer on the counter, feeling around for his emergency pack of cigarettes.

All around him, clutter and trash. Tom had been clearing out closets and dressers, the garage and cupboards for weeks—it all had to go—even though Tom wasn't sure why. Had this been a character he was writing, Tom might say this desire to clean house was an attempt to cleanse a muddled mind. Except Tom Hazuka wasn't writing anything these days.

"Why are you calling so late?" Tom struck a match and inhaled a stale Marlboro Red. He flicked the still-lit match in the direction of the cleaning chemicals and roof rat poison boxes spilt across the mosaic floor, tempting fate to ignite.

"What am I supposed to do?" Alan said. "You don't return my calls. For all I know, you've gotten drunk and run yourself off the road. Or killed somebody." There was a pause. "It's serious this time, Tom."

With Alan, it was always "serious."

"Pearlman's dropping you. They want the money back."

At least once a year, Tom received this threat from Alan. The latest publisher in a long line was cutting ties. He'd have to return the advance, which everyone damn well knew he'd spent long ago.

"I'll have a draft by the end of next week," Tom said, tipping back his head and draining the bottle.

"There is no next week. Not this time."

"This is what you get paid to do as my agent—"

"I'm not calling as your agent; I'm calling as your friend." Alan sighed. "You could've been something special," he muttered. "One of the great mystery writers of all time. When *Murder by Millions* came out, I said to myself, 'There it is—the birth of a genius.' It's why I stuck around through the sub-par follow-ups and increasingly long droughts, across all the wives and DUIs, because I knew you had a rare talent. There's no telling how far you could've gone."

"I'm fine where I am."

"Sure. Mesa Community Tech. The dream of every great author."

"You think this is easy!" Tom shouted. "Do you know the pressure to continually top yourself? To find more imaginative ways to murder people?"

"Tom, the truth is they've got some new editors up here, and they aren't exactly fans of your brand of armchair detective fiction. They want fresh blood. You would've had to dazzle with this next offering for them to even consider keeping you. But the drunkenness. The lack of production. Pearlman is looking to the next generation."

"Next generation?" Tom had to laugh. "I work with the next generation *every day*. And let me tell you. There isn't one. No attention to story or craft—"

"Sorry to be the bearer of bad news, old buddy. Get some sleep. And, really, think about checking yourself in somewhere. You need to—"

Tom slammed the receiver into its cradle.

Mutherfuckers. Drop him? Without the Hazuka name, Russell Pearlman would be running copy for some advocacy rag.

Tom's head throbbed. He ransacked the opened cupboards until he found an old bottle of holiday brandy tucked in the back, then returned to his desk to try to assign a letter grade to varying degrees of butchery.

Alan and Pearlman had it wrong. His drinking wasn't the problem: he drank to deal *with* the problems. After all, what is a writer who doesn't write?

Tom picked up a portfolio. Perfect.

Alexander Pincher.

How many semesters did this make? Four? Five?

If any one student was indicative of the severe downturn Tom Hazuka's life had taken, it was Alexander Pincher.

Alexander had been a thirty-one-year-old undergrad when he first signed up for Tom's intro writing course at Mesa. Cadaverous, gangly, with a mass of tangled black hair and sparse beard in patches, Alexander was forever sporting outdated T-shirts from marginal '70's rock bands like Styx and REO Speedwagon. He'd come up to Tom that first day, overly enthusiastic, the sort of Chatty Cathy whose desire to please grates with each surmounting, pointless word.

"I can't believe it," Alexander had said, beaming bright. "Tom Hazuka. *The* Tom Hazuka. How fortuitous the fates have brought us together."

Fortuitous. The kind of ten-cent word Tom Hazuka abhorred.

"I'm going to be a great mystery writer, too," Alexander said.

Alexander Pincher was a terrible writer. To say he didn't understand the basic tenets of mystery writing is to test the boundaries of the word "understatement." Hell, Alexander didn't understand how to construct a single grammatically sound sentence. Every story he wrote the same, a dreadful blend of post-apocalyptic wastelands and sci-fi (a genre Tom despised), whose hero, some misunderstood, time-traveling detective, scours assorted wormholes and vortexes in search of a never-seen, dastardly madman hell-bent on universal domination. Yet, somehow, though the fate of the entire galaxy hangs in the balance, the story manages to be completely devoid of plot.

His first semester with Alexander, Tom was really trying. He'd convinced Caroline (ex-wife number three) to reconcile, his drinking was under control, and big things were expected from him at Pearlman.

So Tom tried to teach Alexander, who did have a couple attributes working in his favor. Alexander was older than most students, for one, and Tom soon discovered the kid had plenty of real world experience upon which to draw.

Orphaned at a young age, Alexander grew up with a New England aunt, his only family, until she died when he was eighteen, at which point he set out to explore America. And he had, hopping freighters across the heartland, working odd jobs, everything from gas station attendant in Duluth to stable boy in El Paso. These were exciting stories, Tom implored, grounded in reality.

Mystery, Tom said to him, doesn't have to be that mysterious. Human passions are simple but strong. Crime and murder are the result of that relationship stretched to unstable heights.

At these lessons, Alexander would emphatically nod, say he got it, but the next story would be more interplanetary gobbledygook.

Tom gave him a generous C that first semester and sent him on his way.

So he'd been a little surprised to see Alexander next semester, once again signed up for his introductory workshop.

That was the semester when everything started falling apart. Tom's writer's block grew worse. Alan started hounding him. Caroline headed back to New York. Tom drank. The blackouts began, days, nights blurred. Months melted off the calendar.

The one constant through it all (besides the bottle) was Alexander Pincher.

Every day. Before class. After class. Every semester. Tom once even gave him an A, hoping he'd go away. But he didn't. Whereas everyone else (including Tom himself) couldn't stand Tom's company, Alexander never seemed to tire of it. When Tom stopped keeping office hours, Alexander would track him down at Wounded Knee, the bar halfway between campus and Tom's house.

Tom had met with him there last week, in fact, before the final class, although, as usual, Tom could only vaguely recall the details. Tom didn't remember how he even got home that night but figured he must've driven because his car was in the driveway the next morning.

Alexander hadn't attended the last class, and Tom had been relieved. In his faculty mailbox was Alexander's portfolio.

The way Tom arranged his classes, each student work-shopped a story or two during the semester, which he or she then turned in at the end, along with a new, unseen piece.

Tom begrudgingly opened Alexander's portfolio. There was a note.

Dear Professor Hazuka,

Thank you for all your help. I will not be taking your class anymore. I am dropping out of college. I hope you like my last story. It's called Red Pistachios. I couldn't have written it without our talk.

Sincerely,

Alexander Pincher

The new piece that followed, Red Pistachios, was a long, long story, but at least Tom had managed to teach the boy how to write a coherent sentence after five semesters (no easy task), and (thankfully) this time the action took place on planet Earth.

And it could've been the booze—dare he say it? There were almost bona fide moments of... competence.

Red Pistachios was about a serial killer, an unnamed, frustrated mystery writer who decides to put his expertise into real world practice. The serial killer genre had never been one of Tom's favorites, having been drubbed to bits. But Alexander's piece was palatable, the tone almost playful, a radical departure from previous endeavors, and there was a tangible arc. Actual plot points, from a first murder of necessity to the transition when a taste for the flesh is acquired. It flowed, at times proving almost gripping, balanced between absurdity and retrospection, depth and brevity.

The nameless hero in the piece is destined to go down in the murderous annals, surpassing Bundy, Ramirez, Dahmer. He may never get caught. Except for one fatal flaw: he loves red pistachios. He can't stop chomping on them. And so, at every scene, he leaves behind fingerprints.

The notion of the perfect killing machine undone by such a simple, foolish turn made Tom laugh out loud.

What happened next for Tom was fuzzy. Because of the blackouts, Tom could never be sure what he actually did and what had been filled in by the mind trying to connect the dots of time.

Tom had been drinking throughout reading Alexander's story, and though he found himself intermittently engrossed, there was no denying he *was* drunk. After reading the part about the red pistachios, Tom succumbed to uncontrollable bursts of laughter. When one is that drunk, it's easy to find inane humor in the nonsensical. Although Tom seriously doubted Alexander intended the piece to be so funny, it was. A serial killer who loves red pistachios! In fact, the more Tom ran the ludicrous notion through his head, the harder he'd laugh—the idea so absurd, *his* life so absurd, his gut literally aching.

Tom would later hazily recollect grabbing a manila envelope and scribbling out the name "Russell Pearlman" on the front, and slipping Red Pistachios inside, along with a note, scrawled in big, block letters.

Dear Russell,

Here is the future of mystery writing. Go fuck yourself.

Sincerely,

Tom Hazuka

Or something to that effect. After which, Tom could've stumbled out his front door, sealed manila envelope in hand, repeating the phrase "red pistachios" over and over, until the very sound of those consonants and vowels would've deconstructed to the point that they no longer sounded like real words.

The Arizona sky might've shimmered clear and cloudless, a rosy wash of purple and crimson with the new day's rising, the Saguaros lining the block, a nip to the air.

Tom never remembered actually putting the envelope in the mailbox.

He awoke in the wet Bermuda grass of the lawn.

* * *

Tom rang the English Department the next morning, told the secretary to give everyone in his classes a B and to tell the chair that he quit. Tom then drove to the liquor store, picked up enough alcohol to drink himself into a coma, locked the doors and pulled the blinds. He unplugged the telephone, and got started.

Tom couldn't tell how many days passed. Like an eclipse, thin strips of light blazed around the drawn shades, signifying one day's ending, before darkness returned to consume him. Nothing was real, dreamscapes tempered with fleeting moments of lucidity.

It could've been a week or two. It could've been more. But one day, Tom heard a relentless banging on his door. When he managed to open it, there stood Alan, hat in hand, ear-to-ear smile, frantically waving a stack of papers.

"You did it!" Alan said, breezing past. "Don't know *how*—but you did it!— How can you see anything in here?" Alan flipped on the lights to reveal what looked like a refugee outpost, floor strewn with empty bottles of bourbon, whiskey, and scotch, crumpled cigarette packs and crushed beer cans.

"What are you doing here?" Tom's head felt thicker than over-cooked oatmeal.

"Your phone's not work—" Alan stopped, catching a good glimpse of Tom's face. "Jesus, what have you been doing? You look like you've been through chemo!"

Tom reached up to feel the bones of a skeleton. He couldn't recall the last time he'd eaten solid food. Tom found a bottle with something left and slumped into the chair, gesturing with a limp arm. "If you'll be so kind, I have to get back to work."

"I don't know how you're doing it in this condition—but who am I to mess with genius? Writers, eh?" Alan chuckled. "How much longer?"

"How much longer what?" Tom threw back the bottle.

Alan shook the sheaf. "Until you finish. Pearlman wants this padded to book length, stat."

"What are you talking about?"

Alan tossed the manuscript onto the couch. It was Alexander Pincher's typed story, Red Pistachios.

Alan took a seat opposite him. "I hate to admit it, but I'd given up on you. I would've been shocked to see you produce *any*thing, let alone something as fresh, as irreverent—as bitingly satirical—as this."

Tom picked up the manuscript, held it between forefinger and thumb, as though it were a giant turd. "You've read this?"

Alan's face screwed up. "*Of course.* Everyone at the house has. Pearlman called me the moment he finished. They are ecstatic!"

"Pearlman... *likes* it?"

"Likes it? Tom, you have reinvented the genre with this story!" Alan leaned forward. "If there was one knock against even your best work, let's face it, you've never been a particularly funny writer. It takes a lot of *chutzpah* to poke fun at yourself like you have here. A washed-up mystery writer turned serial killer. Ha!"

It hadn't dawned on Tom that Alexander was taking a poke at him. The little prick.

Tom pushed himself up and headed to the kitchen for some water. He could feel his bloated liver protesting, pushing aside lesser organs. He couldn't process what was happening.

"Would it kill you to show a little joy?" Alan mockingly pleaded. At the sink, Alan snapped the blinds, which caused Tom to shield his eyes like a vampire.

"It's been a rough time," Tom said, bringing a glass to his chaffed lips.

"Maybe this will help." Alan slid an envelope along the counter.

Tom picked it up and peered inside. There was a check from Pearlman. It was a large check. "What is this for?"

"*That* is how excited Pearlman is. He wants to renew your contract. Pearlman believes—and I agree—this is the one that puts you back on the map."

Red Pistachios? Tom couldn't believe he was saying those words in conjunction with restarting his career. A story written by the worst writer in North America. He half expected someone to pop out of the dishwasher with a hidden camera.

Alan firmly clasped a hand on Tom's shoulder. "Who says you can't teach an old dog new tricks?"

* * *

That afternoon, Tom flew up to New York with Alan. Pearlman insisted on seeing him in person. After a shower and shave, a hot meal, Tom felt almost felt human again.

Tom brought Red Pistachios with him on the plane and re-read it, sober. He had to admit, it was genuinely funny. In parts. Tom couldn't quite see the literary value in it that Pearlman and Alan had, but he had to hand it to Alexander; it wasn't half bad. Somehow in suffering through all those semesters and myriad private lessons, Tom had managed to teach the kid how to write after all.

Entering Pearlman Publishing was a hero's welcome. Everyone stopped to shake his hand and congratulate him. There was a spread of fresh cold cuts and tiny breads. Tom didn't get it. It wasn't *that* good of a story, and it certainly wasn't finished—but

Tom would be lying if he said all the attention didn't touch a part of him that desperately needed some touching.

The meeting with Pearlman went well. Initially, it wasn't so much a meeting as it was a long apology "for ever having doubted a man of Tom Hazuka's remarkable abilities."

Eventually, Tom reassured him all was forgiven.

The only hitch came when Tom tried to pitch his new ideas for the book, the ones he had begun brainstorming, ways in which to soften the more ludicrous elements. At each of these suggestions, Pearlman and Alan would grow uneasy, saying that of course it was *his* book, before gently persuading the author to stick closer to the source material.

A lack of the drink caused Tom's hands to shake, and a headache soon returned, so Tom finally agreed, just to get out of there and back to his hotel room and its fully stocked mini-bar.

But a funny thing happened once Tom got back to that room. After a couple shots, his mind suddenly cleared, and he knew what had to be done. Tom began rewriting on the spot. Months and months of writer's block vanished. And as he hastily scribbled onto the manuscript and added pages, Tom got the strangest sensation. He anticipated the turns, the twists, instinctively knew the dialogue that would naturally flow out of these characters' mouths before he even wrote it.

It was as though the story *were* his.

* * *

A year and a half later, the book came out. It was reviewed by the *Times*, among others. Very favorable reviews. Alan booked Tom to appear on talk shows, after which the author was slated to do a full tour. Tom was flying back and forth to New York so often that he put his Arizona house up for sale. Tom Hazuka was out of exile.

Now, Tom Hazuka was not a stupid man. Following that first meeting in New York, he made several inquiries to locate Alexander Pincher. But, true to his word, Alexander had dropped out of Mesa. Tom knew the boy didn't have any family—he couldn't imagine he had many friends—and given his history of travel, Alexander could've gone anywhere. The guy was probably working on some farm in Minnesota by now, writing more woeful tales of

Captain Planet. And who was Alexander Pincher, really? Let's face it, the guy got lucky. Alexander had simply proven the old adage: he was the monkey left alone in a room with the typewriter long enough.

Tom knew that one day Alexander may well stumble upon the book. In fact, it was likely. But what could he do about it? It would be Alexander's word against his. Tom was the writer, the one with the pedigree and name. All Alexander had done was supply a premise, an outline. Tom had done the real work. Sometimes Tom Hazuka even found himself thinking that, after all the drinking he'd been doing, Alexander Pincher had been but a figment of a beleaguered imagination, that the idea for the book actually was his. It is the lies we tell ourselves that keep us living, after all.

Best of all, Tom stopped drinking. Just like that. He was amazed at how effortless it had been, especially given the amount of alcohol he'd consumed those last few years, and he did it without being hospitalized. Men can die from alcohol withdrawal if not properly supervised and medicated. Doctors will tell you what Tom did simply isn't possible. Alcoholics Anonymous would insist that Tom must've been sneaking sips from a secret stash or that he was in denial.

But they would be wrong.

Red Pistachios had freed Tom Hazuka, in more ways than one.

* * *

Friday night and Tom was packing up the last of his boxes. He'd found a place in Manhattan and had even restarted an amiable correspondence with Caroline, which he hoped would blossom into something more once they were in the same city again. The moving truck would be here tomorrow.

Outside, the desert night was hot and dry, but with the air conditioner on full blast, the air inside was chilled arctic cool. Tom noshed on a bag of red pistachios. Ever since the release of the book, he couldn't get enough of the goddamn things.

It was about 10:00 p.m. when Tom heard the knock and crossed the floor, kicking aside unpacked cardboard boxes and tape guns.

And there was Alexander Pincher. In his right hand, a copy of the *Red Pistachios*, his face betraying an expression of severe distress.

Tom Hazuka retained his composure, and cordially invited the boy in.

Alexander didn't say anything as he plunked himself in a chair, book clutched tightly to his bony chest. It looked as if he'd been crying.

Setting his bag of nuts on the end table, Tom asked if he wanted a drink and, before Alexander could answer, headed for the kitchen.

"How did you know where I lived?" Tom asked casually.

"The bar. That last night," Alexander replied with a detached tone. "Drove you home."

Sweat started to bead on the back of Tom's neck. He reassured himself that he had nothing to fear. Alexander Pincher was a thirty-something ne'er-do-well. He didn't matter.

Tom slowly turned over his shoulder. "I figured you'd be hiking the Appalachians by now." Tom forced a laugh.

"The book," Alexander said, still not looking Tom's way. "Need to talk to you about the book."

"Sure, Alexander. We can talk about the book," Tom said, walking to the refrigerator, having to talk louder. "Just wanted to catch up a bit first." Tom opened the fridge, casting aside the leafy greens and rare roasted meats, and retrieved a bottle of grape soda pop. "Where have you been these past few months?"

"Alaska. On a fishing boat."

"When did you get back into town?"

"Tonight."

"Seen anybody else yet?"

"Don't know nobody else," Alexander said. "Came straight from the Greyhound station."

"I didn't hear a cab..."

"Walked," Alexander said.

Including his latest effort, Tom Hazuka had written over fifteen mystery novels, and in every one there had been a murder. Usually several. He'd had his characters shot, stabbed, drowned, strangled, butchered, poisoned, decapitated, and dropped in a vat of acid. Tom's killers were rarely the cold, unfeeling types. Often, they agonized over their decisions (except for the husband who drops his wife in the acid in *Murder by Mince Meat*). These killings were crimes of passion, the purest forms of the basest instincts. No one takes killing lightly. It had always seemed to Tom that a killer, even the most psychotic, on some level understands the magnitude of such conclusive action, thus reaffirming the value of human life.

It comes down to a choice. They simply value their own life more.

So when Tom poured Alexander a glass of pop with his one hand, and reached beneath the sink for the roof rat poison with the other, all the while carrying on a genial conversation, Tom both knew what he was doing, understood the gravity of the situation, while, at the same time, he was far removed from the situation, like a specter floating high above the body of Tom Hazuka.

It was a choice. An artistic choice a writer has to make.

Tom entered the living room and brought Alexander his soda. "You must be thirsty, walking all that way."

Alexander took the tall glass and downed a hearty gulp.

Tom sat across from him, on the sofa.

Alexander took another swallow, and every muscle in Tom's body relaxed.

"I see you've read the book," Tom said, swiping his big bag of red, salty nuts.

Alexander turned to face Tom now, the pink rims of his eyes welling. He held up his copy. "Why didn't you tell me?"

Tom sighed with bored bemusement, popping a pistachio, shell and all. "Alexander, you're still young. There are things that might be hard for you to understand."

"I know I'm not much of a writer," Alexander said, "but what you think means a great deal to me. I look up to you, Professor Hazuka."

"I'm not your professor anymore." Tom grabbed a fistful of nuts.

Alexander hung his head low, casting a sheepish sideways glance. "You know I'd never intentionally steal anything from you."

"'Steal' is such a harsh word, Alex, don't you think—" Tom almost choked on a pistachio. "Steal from... *me*?"

"Never. You're like a personal hero."

"Sorry," Tom said, replaying the exchange, "but what do you mean, 'steal from me'?"

"*Red Pistachios.* I didn't know you were *writing* it when we talked. I thought it was just an idea."

Tom's brow furrowed. "When we talked, when?"

"At the bar. Wounded Knee. The night I drove you home."

"We talked about"—Tom pointed at the book—"*Red Pistachios?*"

"Yes. But I didn't know you were going *to write it*. I just thought it was such a funny idea, you know, a serial killer who loves red pistachios, and I know how sick of my stories you were getting. I thought it was something that came to you that night, you know, 'cause of what we were talking about. At the bar. The bowl on the table."

"We talked about... writing this book?"

"Yeah, remember, I followed you after class? I wanted to talk to you about my final story, and you said, Fine, but we'd have to talk at the bar."

"What did I say again?" Tom asked.

"You know, how I needed to simplify my ideas, start with the basics, that if I wanted to write murder mysteries, I had to understand the crime of murder first. The passion behind it. And the mistake that ultimately gets the killer caught."

"The truth is I don't remember that conversation. At all."

Tom asked Alexander to tell him everything that was said that night.

And so Alexander did. How Alexander had been complaining about not understanding where to start, that the idea of murder seemed so fantastic to him. How Tom said that anyone can be a killer. And when Alexander asked like who, Tom blurted to make the killer a washed-up mystery writer who murders the student who won't leave him alone. How Alexander knew he was joking. How in this particular story, Tom said, the first killing is incidental. Then the killer discovers the power of creation through destruction. The killer develops a taste.

Tom had plotted it all.

Alexander took out a wadded-up napkin from his back pocket and unraveled it. "Don't you remember writing this?"

Tom took the napkin. He recognized the handwriting, the familiar script outlining the arc and resolution, the entire story, start to finish, except the part that trips up our hero.

"And how did you—I mean, I—come up with the twist, what gets the killer caught?" Tom asked.

"There was that bowl of red pistachios on the table?" Alexander replied. "Remember? I asked, 'But what gets him caught?' And you said, 'The simplest mistake, it can be anything.' And then you held up the bowl. 'Red pistachios,' you said. 'Red pistachios get him caught.'" Alexander's ashen face twisted up, as though he were in pain.

The crime is murder. Anyone can kill. The first killing is incidental.

Tom stared down at the napkin, now smudged, smeared with deep red stains from his hands.

Alexander leaned over. "I wasn't trying to plagiarize or anything. When I saw the book in that drugstore in Alaska, I came straight here." The boy doubled over with a grimace. His face turned deathly white. "I don't feel so good. I think I'm actually getting sick over this whole thing, Professor Hazuka."

"Tom," the writer said. "Call me Tom. And no worries, Alexander." He pointed to the half-finished soda. "You're probably dehydrated from the trip. Drink up. Then I'll show you what I am working on next."

COPPERHEAD CANYON

"Because we need the lighter to start a fire or we'll freeze tonight," Emily said.

"I mean, why should I go with him? Send Justin or Rex. Or Deb." Tim glared at his so-called friends, who gawked up from their tents watching the drama unfold on the ridge of Copperhead Canyon. That fucker Kurt down there somewhere. Hotshot college asshole. Some graduation trip this was turning out to be.

"It'll give you a chance to get to know him," Emily said.

"What if I don't want to get to know him?"

"Then you won't be a part of my life. I'm with Kurt now. That's never gonna change."

"Never? How can you possibly say—" Tim kicked at a clay clump. "So that means I have to hike five miles in 100° heat, probably get bit by a copperhead—"

"If you got bit by anything, it'd be a rattlesnake." Emily forced a smile. "We don't have copperheads in Arizona. It's just a name. Like Dead Man's Curve."

"Terrific."

Emily took his hand. "You ever think maybe this is why I broke up with you?"

"Because I don't wanna play Moses with your new boyfriend?"

"No," Emily said. "Because you don't make the most of opportunities when they are presented to you."

The entire trek back to the cars, Kurt wouldn't shut up, not taking the hint when Tim didn't respond to single goddamn thing he said. At least the heat, so unbearable earlier, had given way to cooler afternoon winds, the sun dipping low to cast long shadows over the dry bed and shrubs of the desert floor.

By the time they made the mesa, Kurt and his athletic calves leading the way, Tim decided he was getting in his truck and leaving.

Let these assholes all trying packing into Kurt's Civic tomorrow morning, see how far they get.

"I know all about you and Em," Kurt said over his shoulder as he rifled through his glove compartment. "And I respect that."

I've known Emily since nursery school. Like I need *your* approval.

"Emily is going to need you in her life now more than ever."

What's this jerk talking about?

Kurt held up the lighter, proudly, flipping it to Tim. Then he walked over, looking all sincere and mature. "I want you to know," Kurt said, placing a sympathetic hand on Tim's shoulder. "I'm going to do right by her and this baby."

Walking back through the canyon, Tim felt numb inside. It had turned much colder with the setting sun, all hope of a reunion gone forever. It was wrong. *He* should be the father, just like they always talked about.

A guttural scream bounced off canyon walls.

Tim spun around. Kurt lay on the desert floor, griping his leg, howling in anguish.

The rattlesnake writhed away through the red dust.

"Help me up!" Kurt shouted.

Tim rushed to try and lift him, but Kurt immediately fell back to the ground, crying out and clutching his calf, which was already severely swollen and blistered, oozing gooey white pus.

Tim grabbed his cell, frantically pushing numbers. "There's no reception down here."

"No shit. You'll have to climb back up on the mesa to call." Kurt grit his teeth. "Go!"

Tim ran as fast as he could. This wasn't happening. He'd seen people get bitten by snakes in movies. But this was real life. Tim scurried over boulders and squeezed through narrow passages in the rock. Pictures of Emily getting fat kept popping into his brain, holding up her new baby, beaming.

Tim tried to scale the rocky bank back to the mesa, but his hands shook and he kept slipping.

He slumped against the rocks to catch his breath.

Tim gazed over the valley of Copperhead Canyon, calm washing over him, heartbeat slowing. The desert looked beautiful in the evening gloam, its sky beginning to dance with a million blinking stars coming out of hiding.

Tim reached for his cell but pulled out the lighter instead. He flicked the head, making little sparks, tiny orange fireworks against the purple sky.

He leisurely rose and meandered back in the general direction of the campsite, thinking about good names for a baby.

GO

I'm at the 24-hour Gas 'n' Go out on Old Highway 37, past the boarded-up diner where they sometimes install one of those long-armed, inflatable wacky wavers and sell used cars on the weekend. It's 2 a.m. and pissing rain outside. And cold. Because it's always cold here. Besides the *Frampton Comes Alive* dickwad working the register, I'm the only one in the place. I grab the pregnancy test, bottle of Tums and a six-pack, even though it's actually a few minutes after two, making it illegal to buy booze here. I drop my groceries on the counter and ask for a pack of Marlboro Reds. The seventh time I've quit quitting this month. I can hear my old man, six feet beyond the grave. *I was right about you all along, son.*

Frampton rings me up. He doesn't say anything about the beer. Which is mighty white of him. Then he asks how I'm doing.

How am I doing? I'm buying a fucking pregnancy test at two in the morning at the fucking Gas 'n' Go, how the fuck do you think I'm doing?

I sit in my rust-bucket Buick in the tiny parking lot, killing beers and smoking, staring into the falling rain, the black cornfields lost beyond the turnpike, rain cutting shadows through the headlights, wondering what the hell I'm doing with my life. Half the Gas 'n' Go's sign is burned out, so it only reads "Go." And, brother, I want to.

It's not Trish's fault. I could fertilize brick. Up until now, though, I've been able to convince the others to "do the humane thing." I'm pushing forty. I don't have a bank account because I can't keep a job long enough to make enough money to open one. They keep taking me back at Sherwood to run a one of the dies on the grave-yard, but that's only because I went to school with Kent Chester, who's plant foreman. About a hundred years ago, I kicked Mike Maloney's ass in gym class for picking on him. Don't know why. Didn't even really like Kent. I just hated bullies. Turned out to be the only right thing I ever done. Because Kent always takes me back. Until I show up drunk or call in sick one too many times, and he has to let me go. At which point I collect the unemployment, until that runs out, then it's back to Sherwood long enough to get fired again and start collecting. It's a vicious cycle. Point is, I'm not exactly father material.

But this time I'm screwed. Trish is thirty-five, and she hasn't ever had kids, and I know she wants them. That's a bad combination.

I need to make something happen, so I take a ride downtown, which in my town is a donut shop and a bank, a Dairy Queen that closes every fall and a handful of apartments.

My Buick limps in front of Devlin's building. I know he'll be up. Devlin is always up.

"That's tough, brother," Devlin says, frantically slapping at buttons. "Same thing happened to Sandy's cousin Randy last month. Must be something in the air."

He's playing video games on his computer, headset wrapped around his hairless lumpy head like he's a real pilot.

Devlin's one of these bald guys who started losing his hair when he was in his teens and now he shaves it all off like he intended for it to be that way. Everything in his place looks high class but I know for a fact most of it is from the IKEA over in Somerdale because his brother-in-law works there and trades the shit customers return for drugs. That's what Devlin does. Deals. Pot mostly. Some pills. Not too much of the harder stuff, although I've seen him with an eight ball of coke before. But I'm not here to score.

"I need money," I tell him.

"Who doesn't?"

I keep staring at the back of his head until he gets uncomfortable enough to put down his controller. He spins around in his chair and passes me the pipe.

"OK," he says, with a half smile. "I may have something."

"I ain't delivering dope," I say as I inhale.

"You're busting my balls, man." He snatches back the pipe. "No dope. One of my girls needs a ride. Corbett flaked. Give you $150, plus the girl will probably kick you down something—but I can't promise that."

"Make it $200."

This is Devlin's other enterprise. But it's not what you think. It's not like he's a pimp or anything. Where we live isn't the kind of place where you see girls standing on street corners downtown. Devlin's got a bunch of girls doing the college thing up at State, so he places these ads in the back of the *Express*, and then old guys too pathetic to get any on their own pay for a girl to come over and shake her ass. But that's all she does, dance, and maybe if she feels like it she'll rub one out for the poor bastard. That's how Devlin described it, anyway.

I'm not thrilled, but Devlin says it shouldn't take any longer than an hour, and I'm certainly not in any rush to get back to Trish. Plus, I could use the time to think, come up with a plan of action.

The girl's name is Cassie. At least that's what she tells me. I doubt it's her real name. She's pretty enough, a little on the chunky side, like she hasn't quite shed all her baby fat or the freshman fifteen, but her face looks like a manic-depressive clown did her make-up, all pancake blush and sparkle eyes. She insists on sitting in the back, like I'm some creepy old dude who can't resist making a pass at any twenty-year old who sits next to him. I guess I can't blame her. When I was twenty and I'd see people my age, I'd wonder why they didn't put a bullet in their head and end it already.

I'm supposed to take her up to the Ridge, where they have all those ancient colonial knockoffs with the giant columns and hire people to mow their football field-sized lawns. My father used to mow those lawns. Before he dropped dead my sophomore year of high school. My job is to walk her up to the guy, let him see that she's not alone. I pointed out to Devlin that I'm not exactly built like a bouncer but even he brings up the Mike Maloney story, because by now it's sort of legendary around here. I mean, I *did* knock the guy out with one punch, hitting him so hard he literally pissed his pants, which in the 11th grade sort of makes you a bad ass. Maloney ended up dropping out, not even graduating. You piss yourself in high school, in a tiny town like ours, you'll never hear the end of it. That's your legacy. I heard he ended up getting drunk one night and trying to cross the turnpike and got hit by a car, dead.

I'm wondering how much all this is costing. Because if I'm getting two bills, it's got to be a lot, which seems weird for just dancing, because you could probably drive into the city and get a lot more for your money, but, hey, it's none of my business, and now I see the town is doing some work on the underpass by the trestles because it always floods there in the spring, and that must've been good shit I smoked at Devlin's, my ears are ringing like a mutherfucker, and what the hell do I care what this girl is doing? As long as I get my two hundred bucks. I'm still hoping I'm going to be able to convince Trish to... do the humane thing.

"Where you know Devlin from?" the girl asks from the back, which startles me out of my head.

I fish out another Percocet. "Same way you know anybody." I catch her looking at me funny in the rearview, like I'm lying. "I buy pot from him sometimes. Why, where do you know him from?" Which is kind of immature of me, I admit.

Cassie turns away. I push the lighter, tap another smoke. The cops are never prowling out here this late. Still, I keep the car steady. Last thing I need is another DUI.

"Can I have a cigarette?"

I slide one up. She reaches over the seat, plucks it.

"You really shouldn't be smoking," I say, though I don't know why. What the hell do I care if she smokes?

"Thanks, *dad*," she says, and plops back.

I catch her eyes again in the mirror, and the longer I look, the younger she seems.

"Why aren't you sleeping?" Cassie asks, blowing the smoke out her heavily primped mouth.

"What we playing? Twenty questions?" Which is stupid. It's something my father used to say, and comes out automatically.

I turn up Worthington, the quiet streets lined with pretty oaks and maples.

She screws her mouth, sucks in the smoke and blows it out the side slowly, affecting a grown-up pose and staring at me intently.

"My girlfriend thinks she might be pregnant," I say. "We got in a fight, and she had me pick up a test, but I'm not in any rush to get back and find out. Satisfied?"

"I don't want to have kids," Cassie says.

"Ain't too high on my priority list right now either, sweetheart, believe me."

"That's it," Cassie says, pointing at one of the big square colonials towering along the Ridge.

I turn up the long driveway.

"You can let me out here," she says.

"I'm supposed to walk you in."

"It's all right," Cassie says, "I know this guy. Besides, you never have any trouble when you show up, only when you're leaving." She pulls out her cell. "Give me your number. I'll text you when I'm done."

"I don't have one."

"You don't have a number?"

"Yeah, I have a number. I don't have a cell. I got a regular *house* phone. But you can't call that, can you? Because I'm sitting here."

"Who doesn't have a cell phone?"

"I don't."

"Come back in an hour," she says.

I start another half-ass protest, but Cassie grabs her purse and is out the door, hugging herself and rubbing her arms because it's freezing. I watch her tight little rear end bouncing along in that mini-dress she's got painted on.

I light a new cigarette and look around, eyes adjusting to the darkness. The Ridge is as good as it gets. Small town rich. Big house. Two-car garage. Being able to pay some college girl to shake her ass for you in her star girl pants. The American Dream.

I retrieve a warm beer from under my seat, and blast the heat. By now it's gotta be almost 4 a.m., but I have no way of knowing for sure because my radio doesn't work, and I must be tired from all the beers and the heat, the pot and the Percs, my eyelids feeling heavy, and I must've fallen asleep, because suddenly I wake in a panic. It's getting light out and Cassie hasn't come back.

Fuck.

I get out the car and jog up the walkway, these perfectly placed stones cutting a path through immaculate landscaping, and go around the side of the big brown house. There's a light on, and I can hear music playing inside. I look in the window, and at first I don't see Cassie, only two boys who look like they are fifteen sitting at the dinning room table, and now I know they are in high school because they're wearing varsity jackets, and on the table is a pile of white, which they are cutting into lines with a credit card. I don't know what I find more offensive, that the little pricks are doing coke at that age, or that they are wearing their goddamn varsity jackets inside. Then I see Cassie, who comes in from the other room. She's wearing nothing but a pair of panties, pert little titties jiggling, and one of the high school dicks pulls her on his lap, where she giggles and leans over, snorting a rail. Then he pushes her head down, and she disappears under the table.

"Hey!" I say, knocking on the glass.

Everyone looks up.

I run around the side of the house. A door is cracked open. I shove it in.

"What the fuck?" one of the boys says, as he stands and zippers up.

Cassie's crawled out from under the table, her clown makeup smeared. She tugs at his arm. "It's all right," she says. "This is the guy who drove me here. He's cool."

"Cool," the boy says, sitting back down with his buddy. He holds up a dollar bill straw. "You party?"

"No, I don't fucking *party*," I say. "How old are you? Whose house is this?"

"It's my *parent's* house, man," the other one says. "They're in Mexico. And what do you care?"

What *do* I care? I shouldn't give a shit. But I do. I don't know why, but something about seeing a bunch of high school kids snorting drugs and having some kind of a sex orgy strikes me as, y'know, wrong.

I take Cassie by the arm. "Come on, we're going."

One of the boy stands, yanks her back. "Fuck you are, old man. We already paid."

"I don't give a shit." And I push him. Hard.

Then they're both on me, varsity jacket fists flying fast. I can't get out of the way. I try to put my hands up, but I get clocked on the chin good, and then I'm falling down. I must've blacked out, because next thing I know I'm looking up at three faces staring down on me, and everyone looks really concerned.

Then Cassie covers her mouth and points at my crotch, and now I feel the warm puddle spreading beneath my balls.

"Holy shit," one of the boys says, laughing. "The old guy pissed his pants."

* * *

The rain's cleared, clouds swept away, cold sun up, and I'm racing to get back to my apartment, which is only a couple miles down the hill, but it feels a world away. I need to get back to Trish. Despite my hangover and getting cold cocked, I'm finally seeing things clearly. They talked about this at one of those meetings the judge made me go to after the last DUI. They call it... fuck, I don't remember what they call it. But they talk about it a lot, how there are just, like, these moment when you start seeing things for what they really are.

I run up the apartment steps, burst through the door, and she's just as I left her, sitting on my ratty couch. She peers up. It looks like she's been crying.

"Where have you been?" she asks. But she doesn't sound mad, more like she's... bored.

"All the stores were closed."

"Why's your mouth bleeding?" She wrinkles her nose. "You smell like bum piss."

"Forget about that. Listen. We should keep the baby."

"What?"

"The baby. We should keep it. I know it sounds crazy, but I really think this could work. I know we've only known each other a few months—"

Trish covers her face in her hands and starts crying harder.

"Why are you crying? I just said we should keep it."

Trish wipes her eyes, stands and grabs her coat and handbag off the milk crate end table and makes for the door.

"Where are you going?"

"I got my period while you were getting stoned with your buddy, Devlin."

"I wasn't getting stoned."

"What would make you possibly think you are ready to have a kid?" She holds up her hand like she's about to start listing things off. And then she starts listing things off. "You're thirty-nine, you don't have a job, you've got a drug problem—"

"I don't have a drug problem."

"You've got a drug problem. And an alcohol problem. And a *life* problem. You're not exactly father material." She makes herself laugh. "I'm sorry. I shouldn't have said that. It's been a long night."

Trish walks over and kisses me on the forehead, like I'm a little boy with a boo boo. "You should sleep it off."

Then she's gone.

And now the new-day light is shining brightly through my windows, because all I have for curtains are the old threadbare towels I've hung, which are worn so thin you can literally see right through them.

I sift through the clutter on the kitchen table, looking for a cigarette to smoke because in my rush to get upstairs I left the pack in the car, and for some reason the thought of going back outside in the sunlight right now fills me with a dread I can't stomach. But I can't find an ashtray with any butts because I emptied them all when I quit yesterday morning. Instead all I find are the stacks of red-letter bills that I haven't opened in ages.

I step over the empty beer bottles and spread-out piles of dirty laundry on the floor, the balled-up, oily McDonald's wrappers, and head into the kitchen, which in my tiny apartment is only about six feet away. Just as I open the fridge, the lights go out.

I can't believe this shit.

Bitch drank the last beer.

THE EXTERMINATOR

When I arrive, police cars are already there and a man is snapping pictures in the hot early morning sun, and I know it is her before I see the yellow tape stretched around the palms and poles like saltwater taffy. I spot the coroner, the gurney with the sheet pulled over the body, the blood seeping into the fibers. Everything slows down. Even though I've done nothing wrong, I want to turn around, get back in my van, drive far, far away. But there is nowhere to run. When you have a record like mine you are going to be questioned, sooner or later.

I hear the detective say, "Bring me the Bug Man."

* * *

They call me the Bug Man.

If you live in South Florida, you have bugs—silverfish, sugar ants, termites, roaches. I've become an expert on roaches. You have your American roaches, your brown-banded roaches, smoky-brown roaches, German roaches, and palmetto bugs, which are still cockroaches, just a lot bigger. Sometimes they're called skunk roaches because they smell so bad. Word is the hissing cockroaches will be here soon.

* * *

The sun had just come up Saturday morning when I pulled my van onto the curb and parked in front of the Seaside, a slummy apartment complex on Ocean Avenue, but it was already hot. When I stepped outside, I could feel my shirt stick to my biceps and back.

A faded art deco that sat behind a murky green pool, Seaside stood on a lesser strip of Ocean Ave., one that wasn't as sexy as the rest of South Beach. Tall palms with giant fronds and overflowing big blue garbage bins blocked a view of the sea. It stank like gym socks left in a hot trunk.

The apartments weren't far from ritzy Lincoln Road, but in Miami you go block to block. High class never far from the hell of Little Haiti.

I watched the lowlifes lurking in the sawgrass and monkey-brush as I made my way up the walkway. Windblown sands made it feel like I was walking on sandpaper. On the second floor landing, greasy men, arms slung through the bars, scratched themselves and drank from paper bag 40s, women, long past their prime, selling the only thing they had left. A Cuban with a black eye patch stepped in from out of the shadows.

There aren't many jobs available to a man like me when he gets out of a place like Okeechobee. But there are always bugs in South Florida that need exterminating.

Last time I'd been at the Seaside no one was living in 5A.

This time, she was.

Young, tiny like a bird, a finch or maybe a quail, dark skin, she had the body of a teenager, tight, no curves.

Her eyes looked... troubled.

I hit the bathroom, opened the back door and squirted the little patio where pepper plants grew in round pots. A stiff ocean breeze blew back some boric acid, which stung my eyes and made them tear up. They began to burn and I closed them tight. I felt something placed in my hands.

I wiped my eyes with the handkerchief she'd handed me. Red, silk, with a monogrammed letter "S."

"Sarhina," she said, as I returned the handkerchief to her. She touched my hand. "I'm about to make coffee. Would you like to stay for some?"

It's easy being insulted, having someone be cruel, but when someone is nice to me, it saws like a dull knife on raw bone.

"Maybe next time," she said with a sad smile.

Walking back to my van, I felt the sun beat down on my back, burning through to my skin. The harsh glare smacked off the asphalt in shimmering waves, making it hard to see. I shielded my eyes.

Across the street, the Cuban with the black eye patch stood watching me. I'd seen him before, this Cuban. So I eyed him back.

At my feet, a fat palmetto bug skittered past. I stomped it with my heel, and it popped like an overripe berry.

* * *

"Where were you last night, between midnight and two a.m.?" Detective Kaplowitz wants to know.

Sleeping.

"Anybody verify that?"

No.

"What were you in Okeechobee for?"

He already knows the answer to that.

"Never mind," Kaplowitz says, pointing down at the thick binder on the table. "Got everything I need to know right here."

And so on. I could do this drill in my sleep.

* * *

When I got off work that night, I took a long, cold shower, but I couldn't shake Sarhina from my brain. What was a girl like her doing living in the Seaside? And why had she asked a man like me, a 6'4" longhair covered in ink, to stay? Stepping out of the cold water back into the heat, I felt lightheaded, and had to grab the edge of the sink to keep from falling down.

I toweled off and poured a drink. I started to get a picture in my head, which got clearer with each slug. When she'd taken my hand, she wasn't asking me to stay for coffee. She was asking for my help. She was caught up in something, desperate enough to take a chance on a stranger. I thought back to the Cuban with the missing eye, how he'd been watching me go in and out of her apartment, how uneasy it had made me feel. Now I knew why.

It was time to go back to work.

Closing in on midnight, I hoisted my canister on my shoulder and climbed back into my van with the tools of my trade. Even at that hour, the night was sweltering, my long red ponytail writhing around the back of my neck like a mean swamp snake. I headed out of Hialeah, making for 95 and the Causeway, as I went scouring the black backstreets of filthy Miami.

When you are good at your job, you can use more than one sense, sniff out the faintest odor, let the hairs on your arm stiffen, tune into the silent cries of a cityscape, and it will point you in the right direction. I'd been exterminating bugs all my life, from the drunken trailer parks of my childhood, through those long, dark nights inside Okeechobee, good deeds misconstrued and perverted, until those insects came creeping out of the stone, squiggling over the dirty floor, thousands of the diseased little fuckers, and I'd have to jump down, stomping, grinding, punching the walls, until each one was dead...

I knew where to find him. Like all cockroaches, he'd shy from the light, scurrying into the dimmest corners where he thought he'd be safe with all the other vermin.

But this is what I do. I am the Bug Man.

I followed as he caught a bus, dropped off in the skeleton shantytowns of Little Haiti, no doubt looking for something to breed with. I parked my van under a lush eave of bougainvillea, and put on my gloves, strapped on my tank. Only sporadic light shone from power generators inside little huts, cast over the remains of headless chickens and wing bones, sweet starches perfect for scavenging.

Behind the tin shed and oil drums, I pouched, a fast, fluid strike. His body flattened, and I pinned a long, spiny leg to the earth as he writhed to break free, mouthparts flicking every which way, squealing and hissing as I inserted the nozzle deeper inside his throat, filling the cavity. He spasmed and twitched. I cracked my tank against his mandible, and ground it into the mud. Then he spasmed and twitched no more.

I rolled the bloated body down the culvert with the rest of the discarded goat and pig carcasses.

I looked down at the black eye patch I held in my bloody palm. He can't hurt you no more, Sarhina...

* * *

Detective Kaplowitz stands up, puts his hands on the back of the chair. "We know you were there."

I sprayed for bugs.

"But you can't account for why witnesses place your van outside the Seaside shortly after midnight last night. A man with a history like yours—"

I was protecting her.

"Protecting her? From who?"

I tell him about the Cuban with the missing eye, not what I'd done to him, of course, because there is no reason, but about how scared she'd been, how she'd asked for my help, how he'd been stalking her, how I was one of the good guys, couldn't he see that?

Kaplowitz pauses, seeming momentarily stunned, then he smiles weakly, says he'll be right back.

When he returns he is not alone.

My whole body tenses. I fight to break free from the handcuffs, which cut into my wrists and pinch my circulation until my hands swell with blood like giant crustacean pinchers and go numb, my eyes beginning to tear up. He just stands there, a ghost.

"This is Detective Gonzales," Kaplowitz says, putting his arm around the Cuban with the black eye patch. "He was at the crime scene this morning. I think you might be getting... confused. You have a history of getting confused, don't you?"

I was protecting her. Why can't you see that? Tears stream down my cheeks.

"Sure, you were," says Kaplowitz. "Just a question of who you were trying to protect her from."

The Cuban with the black eye patch reaches into his pocket, pulls something out and places it in my hands.

I stare down at the red handkerchief with the pretty letter "S" stitched into the silk.

My skin begins to crawl, as though with a thousand unseen bugs, and my throat starts to close. I feel the choke of boric acid firing down my nasal passageways and esophagus, asphyxiating me. I want to scream but know no sound would come out.

You can't kill them all, no matter how hard you try. More just keep coming. They fuck and they breed, molting their bodies in the darkness, shedding their sickness and assimilating, until they infest us all.

NIX VERRIDA

It had been the Army's psychiatrist who'd suggested he pick up a hobby.

Ray stopped at Y&H on his way home from work, planning to make a quick pit stop for some sectional track. There were other ways to get parts for his model train, catalogues, trade shows, online. He certainly had time at his job to surf the web; it wasn't his ability to move cars that netted him the corner office. But Ray wasn't big on technology, he refused to even own a cell phone, and he didn't trust anything he couldn't hold in his hands. There was no point investing so much time in recreating another world if it wasn't going to be genuine. Since his last tour ended so little seemed authentic anymore.

Several miles off the turnpike, and in the opposite direction from his house, the hobby store was tucked at the end of a long one-lane road, in a giant parking lot across from an out-of-business hamburger stand, the Purple Onion, and an only sometimes-open fishing and tackle shack. It was the one place in the tri-state area where he'd been able to find authentic Ten Wheeler steam trains, even though trips there added an extra hour to his evening commute and left his wife, Bethany, incensed. Everything he did, or didn't do, these days seemed to upset Bethany.

They fought over the baby's being slow to talk; visiting her folks for the holidays; the renovations they'd planned on but now had to put on hold because the life insurance dried up sooner than expected. Ray knew the real reason behind these fights. His wife wasn't a shrew or a bad person. She wanted him to talk about what had happened over there.

You couldn't explain war to someone who's never been. So Ray didn't bother trying. There was a time when he'd had to. After that day at the marketplace, just before his discharge, everyone was ordered by the Army to talk to the head doctors. He was shown pictures of suicide bombers, citizens, insurgents, men who all looked the same, and asked how it made him feel. What difference did it make how he felt? It was four weeks before the whistling in his ears stopped, another six before he could sleep through the night. The man he'd been assigned to talk to was nice. He said kind, gentle things, and Ray knew he was trying to be helpful. The man said talking about it would make it easier. But Ray found that talking about it didn't make anything easier, and it didn't turn back the clock. The dead would always be dead.

The shop's owner, Harold, rapped on the glass inside the store, and Ray popped his head up to catch him pointing at his watch.

"You fall asleep out there?" Harold asked when Ray walked through the door.

"Something like that."

No one else was in the hobby store. Which wasn't uncommon. Even on its busiest days, Y&H didn't draw much traffic. Most of its limited clientele were men like Ray, the lone model train aficionado. Sometimes you saw a father and son. Ray had never been close with his own father. He hoped someday he might bring his boy. It would be nice to share a hobby. Maybe it would draw them closer. The baby was so little now. It was hard to feel close to something so little.

"What you need today, Ray?"

"No. 4 sectional track?" The track was part of the new wye turnout Ray was adding by the outer fixed rails, the gateway into his fictional town, Prescott Falls. Once construction was complete, the X-Terga Dare would embark on her maiden voyage. Everything had to be perfect.

Harold pointed to the side display, where miniature figurines and fauna had been staged along the base of a mountain next to stacks of large grey tubs. "Just got some new scenery in, too."

Almost half an hour passed before Ray walked out of the Y&H. Unable to decide between the county post office and fire station, he got both, but then needed more trees, so he picked up three Eco Deciduous, one sycamore, two maple, throwing in an end tipping wagon for hauling, HC Bull and Co. Ltd. Ray also purchased 2nd radius curved tracking, a Devon Flyer, and four PlotMaster Pedestrian Townspeople. It was the finishing touch of adding the people that proved most satisfying. He selected a pair of soldiers and a jogger in a red track suit; an old woman holding a bag of groceries; and two children, a towheaded boy and girl. He often created backstories for his characters, pairing lovers, children with parents. The towheads would fit in nicely with the baker and his wife beneath the plum trees by the school. They would make a good family.

Driving home, Ray switched on talk radio, which was all he listened to. Music unsettled him. He didn't care what they were talking about as long as it wasn't politics or sports, whose callers and hosts often took to shouting to get their points across. He just liked the talking part. Fishing. Financial advice. Religious programming. Cars. Didn't matter. White noise filling the empty spaces with warm, crackly hums.

Parking in the driveway, he left his bags from the hobby store in the backseat.

"Where have you been?" Bethany held the baby on her hip. It was crying.

"There was traffic."

"Denny made it home fine."

Denny Alderman, Ray's boss and oldest friend, had given Ray the job selling cars on the floor of the showroom, even though Ray had no sales experience and hadn't unloaded a single car in the six months he'd been there. The nice gesture had turned into a headache for Ray, since Denny's wife frequently provided Bethany updates on him.

"I stopped at the hobby store," Ray admitted. "Didn't get anything, really," he added quickly. "Just wanted to see if they'd gotten any new wye tracking in."

The baby kept crying.

"Who's Nix Verrida?" Bethany asked.

"Who's what?"

"Nix Verrida. She's called three times today."

Ray shrugged. "I don't know anybody named... Nick Verrida."

"*Nix* Verrida. That's what the caller ID says. Nix Verrida. A woman. When I finally picked up the third time, she said wrong number."

Ray shrugged.

"Are you going to say anything?"

The baby continued to cry.

"About what?"

The next morning Denny called him into his office.

"You really need to get a cell phone, buddy," Denny said, grinning. "It helps in matters like this, y'know?"

Ray stared, blankly.

"I known you since we were five, Ray. I wouldn't say a word to Melinda."

"About what?"

Denny crinkled a brow. "The woman."

"What woman?"

Denny waited a moment before throwing up his arms. "I told her she was crazy. When the hell would you have time for an affair, in between here and your toy trains?"

"An affair?"

"Mindy was on the phone with Bethany last night when I got home. Some woman had been calling the house all day. Nicki something."

"Nix Verrida."

"Yeah, that's her. Friend of yours?"

"I don't who she is."

Denny drummed his fingers on his paunchy gut.

"I don't know any Nix Verrida," Ray said. "Never met. Never talked on the phone. Never even heard the name until yesterday."

Denny lifted his hands in mock surrender. He tried to look sincere. "How's everything...else?"

"Fine."

Denny's face twisted as though pained trying to hold back the words. Ray encountered this face often. His wife, in-laws, the other guys on the floor. He wasn't stupid. But Ray found it easier to play dumb.

The phone rang and Denny seemed grateful to pick it up. "Yes?" His face turned grave as he cupped the receiver. "For you. Bethany."

Ray reached out.

"She called again."

"Who?"

"Nix Verrida."

"I already told you—"

"She asked for you," Bethany said. "By *name*." The baby cried in the background. "When I asked what it was about, she wouldn't say."

"Maybe it's something to do with work." Ray knew that couldn't be true, and with Denny standing there he felt even worse; he hadn't hooked a single prospective client, let alone reel in an actual sale the entire time he'd been there. "Can we talk about this when I get home?"

"It's not business. She said it's personal."

Ray looked to Denny. "Honey, I'm in Denny's office. This isn't—"

"Do you love her, Ray?"

Ray hung up the telephone.

Denny insisted Ray take the rest of the day off and go work things out with Bethany. There was an undercurrent of admiration in his tone. Even though Ray had never met any woman named Nix Verrida, he decided he was better off letting his friend believe the worst of him. On his way out, Denny patted him on the back. It was without the usual pity.

The mere suggestion that Ray would be having an affair was preposterous. He had neither the time nor the slightest inclination to be intimate with anyone, including Bethany. The notion of sex couldn't be further from his mind. In fact, his libido had been so low since he left the Army, he'd been meaning to make an appointment with Dr. Shapiro to change the medications they had him on. When he thought about it, he honestly couldn't recall the last time he had made love to Bethany.

* * *

The morning of the attack, Ray had been on a rooftop, watching the marketplace through the scope of his M-40. They had been tipped off a few hours earlier about the bomb.

The downtown market scene was unlike anything back in the States. The closest comparison would be a flea market, but one combined with the rabid redneck energy of a monster truck rally or a feeding frenzy at the zoo. Hindquarters of lamb roasted over open-spit fires, spreads of *turshi* and plump dolmas, vats of *bambia* and *harrisa*, steam rising in the dry heat. Merchants hawked fine silks and fabrics, farmers hoisting clay pots and wicker baskets stuffed with figs and pomegranate, sweet dates, okra, lentils, bulghur wheat and barley. Vendors clutching tools pawed at light-skinned passersby, bawling prices and special discounts like carnival barkers, while teams of ragged, barefoot children tugged on solider sleeves, relentlessly.

It had been hot. It was always hot. The sweat ran into his eyes, blurring his vision, but he remained locked and loaded. This was what he was paid to do.

It's the dirty little secret of war. Murder is perhaps the oldest taboo, the ultimate transgression against God. Here not only was it permitted, it was lauded. Ray had never gone to college. But he wasn't ignorant. He knew this was the epicenter of civilization, where it all started, Mesopotamia, Tigress, Euphrates. He knew his Bible. Cain slew Abel, out of Eden he was cast. How many thieves had walked those same dusty roads to the east, condemned for killing? Now killing was his job.

An argument broke out below, two men haggling over meat. Ray knew not to be distracted. He'd seen this before, the equivalent of magical misdirection. Look this way. Where did the rabbit go? Merchants emerged from the shadows to shoo the men away. Ray remained steadfast. A sack of coins fell, splashing across the sands, and the children pounced. The sweat ran in rivulets, salt and dirt tearing his eyes. His hands trembled. A Humvee growled. A young woman crossed Ray's sight. She looked directly at him. Long, straight hair black as a raven. So young, so pretty, so helpless. At that moment, he wished more than anything he could just scoop her up, place them both somewhere safe forever, far from this never-ending hell. A bang. A blast. The marketplace enveloped in a searing flash of white light, and the ground shook. People ducked and scrambled for cover as the old stone walls came tumbling down.

* * *

In the basement, Ray attached his new Spectrum series five-pole motor with dual flywheels. He'd spent most of the day at Y&H, digging through die cast chassis and boilers. He'd been looking for a USRA 2-6-6-2 H-5 locomotive with magnetically operated knuckle couplers, but decided instead on the 4-8-4 Niagara Steam, which was the same line he took with his parents when he was a young boy. It was one of the few happy memories he had from his childhood, gazing out the window at the picturesque scenery rushing by, the warm smells of freshly roasted coffee and gooey pastries filling the dining car.

Ray divided Prescott Falls into two sections: one industrial, the other residential. In the former he installed a concrete mixing plant and an A-Z auto sales kit, replete with 1950's salesman and cars, which sat beside a greasy spoon diner in a long, tin trailer. A sandwich board read Eat at Joe's. The diner was his favorite hangout, stuffed with laughing teenagers, good-natured hooligans in leather jackets, hop sock girls in ponytails. It made him feel young again. Even though he'd grown up in a much later era, something about the nostalgia of the '50s comforted him.

Butted against cornstalks and amber grains, quaint homes had been erected, white fences and kindly neighbors. Pigtailed girls clutched dolls; boys with baseball gloves played catch with their fathers, arms outstretched in anxious anticipation of the ball. Women baked pies. You could almost smell the cinnamon wafting through sleepy, tree-lined streets. There were no hobos in his town.

Driving home late that afternoon, without really thinking about it, Ray had suddenly found himself in Saybrook, driving by the site of the crash.

Ray harbored no ill will toward his mother or father. He didn't think of them as bad people. As their only son, Ray accepted long ago that they probably weren't meant to be parents. When he turned eighteen, he moved away. There were a few holiday cards early on, but finding them forced, Ray stopped responding. And soon there was nothing to answer or return.

The money from the life insurance, though hardly a king's ransom, provided Ray with the resources to take the next step in his life and buy the house. For this he was grateful. But something about the crash bothered Ray, a detail he never shared with anyone, since he knew that if the insurance people thought it was a suicide, they would not pay out on the policy.

Ray couldn't be certain it was a suicide. Just a theory he had. As de facto executor of their estate, he was privy to financial records and bills. His father was out of work. He owed money. They were going to lose their home. And then there was the note.

It hadn't been addressed to Ray or to anyone else. He'd found it among his father's personal effects, written in the old man's hand. It could've meant anything, really. A scrap of paper. One line.

May this bring you peace and happiness.

The old man could've read it on a fortune cookie.

Ray parked by the bridge and got out of his car, peering over the railing into the murky waters below. The accident occurred on a clear night, middle of summer, no rain, no other traffic. He hadn't been drinking. They said his father must've fallen asleep at the wheel. It was 9 o'clock.

Returning home that evening, Ray had found the house dark, Bethany and the boy out. He didn't bother calling her cell to find out where she was, instead heading to the basement to work on his train. The phone rang several times, but Ray did not pick it up.

His wife eventually returned, and he could hear her upstairs putting down the baby.

When the phone rang again, she answered.

Bethany opened the door to the basement. "For you."

Ray wiped his hands on the towel and headed upstairs.

His wife flashed a terse, artificial grin. "It's her."

Ray snatched the receiver. He'd had enough of this. "Good. We'll clear this up right now."

Bethany stepped back and folded her arms.

"Hello?"

"Ray." The woman sounded relieved. There was a hint of an accent, though he couldn't quite place its origin. "I'm so sorry to call you at home."

"Excuse me," said Ray. "Who is—?"

"I didn't know what else to do. I've been so worried."

"I think there's been a mis—"

"When you didn't show up at the diner the other night, I was afraid something had happened. You get so crazy this time of year."

Whatever was going on with this woman, Ray needed to be firm, remove all doubt. He wasn't going to tiptoe around his own house because someone mistakenly dialed a wrong number.

"Miss," he said, calmly. "I am not who you think I am."

"You're upset, darling. I understand. Today is the anniversary of the crash."

Ray's eyes remained fixed on his wife's, and he made sure to keep his expression consistent. His heart sped up. "Excuse me?"

"Your mother and father died today."

Ray ran through his mental calendar. She was right. He hadn't even made the conscious connection when he drove out to the bridge earlier.

"You get so worked up every year about the suicide—"

"What did you say?" Ray felt his esophagus close up, airways choked off.

"I'm sorry, darling. I shouldn't have said that. I know you don't like talking about—"

Ray thumbed the phone off, discreetly. "I understand," he said into the receiver. "Mistakes happen." He waited long enough for her to say good night, then added, "You, too, Miss."

Bethany had a peculiar expression.

"Satisfied," Ray said, handing her back the phone.

As Ray headed down into the basement, his wife looked anything but satisfied.

Ray woke in the morning, helter-skelter on the pullout sofa in the cellar, arms and legs bent in unnatural positions. A bad dream left him panicked, the details already out of reach. He hadn't intended to sleep there, just rest his eyes for a moment; now it was 7 a.m. His eyes burned from thinner fumes.

Bethany and the baby were gone. He made a pot of coffee, quickly showered, dressed, and headed out to his car. His fat unemployed neighbor, Shelby, was watering his prized garden in his robe and offered a wave, which Ray returned sheepishly. The O'Malleys held a 4th of July BBQ every year. Ray always declined the invitation.

At work, Ray ducked into his office and immediately shut the door. He tried not to think of Nix Verrida, or whoever that woman on the phone really was, because when he did start to think about her, his mind would take him somewhere sinister, secret societies, assassins sent to finish the job, bad thoughts he had to work to keep away. He'd begin to sweat, get nervous. Until he'd remind himself that those were crazy ideas. Nobody was after him. It was a wrong number. He reached in his drawer and took his medication. The car crash was a matter of public record. Maybe this woman was from the insurance company and wanted to trip him up. Well, that wasn't happening. No, it was most certainly a case of mistaken identity. She might not even have said the word suicide; it was probably already on his mind, which he knew couldn't always be trusted.

No one disturbed him until quarter till noon, when Denny knocked and poked his head inside.

"You up for lunch?"

"Not really." Ray looked around his desk, which was spotless. "Have some... stuff... I need to catch up on."

"You OK?"

"Fine."

"C'mon," Denny said. "My treat."

"It's not a good time."

"I think you need to come to lunch." Denny's good-natured smile began to fade. "I insist."

* * *

"I hope Chili's is OK?" Denny said, turning in to the restaurant parking lot.

"It's fine," said Ray, who was too preoccupied to notice his wife's car or those of his co-workers, Rick and Billy. Nor did he see his doctor's Lincoln or neighbor's SUV. When he walked in and found Bethany, the baby, Dr. Shapiro, Rick, Billy, and fat Shelby O'Malley, his equally plump wife Rachel and their goofy home-schooled kid, Marjorie, all seated around a big table in the corner greedily swiping chips through giant bowls of salsa and guacamole, it took a moment to process what was happening. Once he did, Ray felt something gnashing fiercely in his gut.

He slowly dragged a chair and scanned the table. Sets of deeply concerned eyes his gaze. How he'd grown to hate that look.

"So what is this?" asked Ray, sitting down, "an intervention?"

"Something like that," Denny said.

"An intervention in fucking Chili's?" Ray spat an unhinged laugh. "For what? Not drinking? Having a hobby? What the *fuck* are you intervening about?"

A few customers looked over. The O'Malleys pulled Marjorie close.

"We all love you, Ray," Bethany said. "We're worried about you."

"Who the hell invited you, Shelby?" Ray said, pointing at his neighbor, then motioning to his wife. "I'm not friends with these people. I live next door to him. And I work with those two." Rick and Billy looked away uncomfortably. "What the hell are any of you doing here?"

"Ray," Dr. Shapiro interrupted, "can you tell me about this woman who has been calling the house?"

"Jesus Fucking Christ! I am not having an affair!"

Customers whispered. Two waitresses loitered nearby. A large black man in glasses, clearly the manager, came to join them. He wore a chili pepper tie.

"Ray, please," Bethany implored. "Keep it down."

"Oh, now, it's Ray please."

"You're causing a scene, buddy," Denny said.

"I'm causing a scene? You drag me down here, spring this shit on me, and I'm causing a scene. Fuck you, Denny."

The O'Malleys gasped.

"And fuck you, too, Shelby." Ray stood up.

Denny reached for his arm, and Ray yanked it away.

The manager took a step toward them and Ray spun, pointed a finger squarely at the man's broad chest like it was a gun, and the manager stopped cold.

"Please, sit back down," Dr. Shapiro said.

"I am not having an affair."

"OK. You're not having an affair," said Bethany.

"I don't know any woman named Nix Verrida!"

"OK. I believe you."

"About fucking time."

"But you've been acting so odd lately, honey. You don't talk to me. You come home and hole up in the basement with your trains. You don't even pay attention to your own son. You look at him like he's a stranger. Sometimes I think you don't even know his name."

Ray looked at the baby. This was ridiculous! Like he didn't know the baby's name. Of course he knew the baby's name!

"Dr. Shapiro—" Bethany looked pleadingly to the doctor—"please, tell him what you told me."

"It's not uncommon, what you're going through."

"And what am I going through?"

"It's called post tr—"

"I'm done listening to this bullshit," Ray said.

"Ray," Bethany said, sternly, "Either you stay and listen to what Dr. Shapiro has to say, or I'm taking the baby and leaving. I mean it. I will be gone tonight."

Ray glowered at her. Then shoved the chair and left without another word.

He hit the steps running, as fast as he could all the way back to the dealership. It was almost two miles. He never broke stride. He could hear his own heart beating, hollow as a tin drum. Jumping in his car, he didn't know where to go. If he were a drinker, this would be a good time to get shitfaced. But the last beer he had was in high school. Never made much sense to him before, why people like his father wanted to get so blotto. He understood it now.

He tore onto the highway, weaving through traffic, navigating around construction, hopped back off, got on the one-lane frontage road, and made for the hobby store. It was the only place he could think to go, but the road seemed stretched out, the ride taking forever. He checked the rearview. No one was following him. That he could see. But the Medhi were crafty.

When he hopped the curb into the parking lot, he immediately saw something was wrong. Weeds sprouted up through cracks in the erupted pavement, giant gaping craters and unsightly erosion. The sign for Y&H was gone, the store boarded up, whitewashed.

Ray jumped out of his car and ran to the front doors, which were held closed with thick chains and a big padlock. He peered through dusty glass. Nothing. Not a trace anyone had ever been there. How could Harold do this to him? He knew Y&H didn't do much business, but he was a loyal customer. The least he could've done was let Ray know. This wasn't fair. You can't just go out of business and not tell someone!

Across the parking lot where the Purple Onion used to be now stood a Chinese restaurant. When the hell did that go up? Ray raced across the shifting, uneven asphalt and pushed through the doors.

There were no customers, just a woman and man, both in Chinese silky pajamas, sitting by the front. The woman stood up and smiled.

"Where's the hobby store?" Ray demanded.

The woman said nothing.

"The hobby store." Ray pointed emphatically out the door. "Over there. Where is it?"

The woman looked confused. "No store."

"I know that!" Ray shouted. "Don't you think I can see that? I'm not stupid. I'm asking you where'd it go?"

"No store," she repeated.

The Chinese man at the table got up. Another, a cook dressed in white, came out of the kitchen.

"What the hell do you know?!" Ray said, swiping a hand over them all. "You're all fucking nuts."

Out in the parking lot, Ray heard helicopters swirling above, but they were too fast, too clever to be caught, ducking safely from view behind trees and clouds, registering just beyond his peripheral. He slowed down and scanned the perimeter. Dead fish stink blew in from the shore. Clearly, they'd been instructed to wait. So he would wait too.

Ray sat in his car and dialed in some talk radio. He closed his eyes.

He awoke in the black of night.

* * *

Before he unlocked the front door, he knew she was gone, could already feel the abandon, like a pall cast. Inside the kitchen, there were no cupboards left open, no baby bottles scooped up in haste, no jackets torn off the hook. The house smelled musty and unlived in. He paused at the refrigerator, gazing at the faded picture of the young boy in a Little League uniform, into dead sunken eyes the same as his own. He opened the door. Mustard, an empty pizza box, some plastic beer rings. Out the window, the O'Malleys' garden was nothing but a tangle of overgrown weeds in the moonlight. How quickly the untended fall apart.

Making for the basement, Ray picked up the phone and absently punched in numbers. A message played that his wife's cell had been disconnected. Maybe he'd gotten the numbers mixed up again.

At the bottom of the stairs, he pulled the string.

The X-Terga Dare lit up. Magnificent.

What had he been so nervous about?

Ray set the phone down and studied his handiwork. All the hours and effort, his meticulous attention to detail had paid off. He'd done it. An entire existence recreated. The schools and factories and mills. The grand houses and fields of promise. So authentic, right down to the little painted numbers on the mailboxes. He knew these people. They were his friends.

He was ready. It was time.

Ray pulled the lever.

Charcoal steam belched into the brilliant new-day sky. The Millers and Stevens waved goodbye to their sons, Charlie and Mack, who were heading off to boot camp, Jane and Jenny Larson standing in knee-highs, watching their boyfriends go, teary-eyed on the platform. They would return heroes.

Up the street, the Plums walked with their twins, Sherry and Bobby, hair so light almost looked white in the morning sun. Earl Sycamore jogged by the post office. Across the street, Agnes Maple carried a sack of groceries, framed by the big red trucks of the fire station.

The clock tower chimed on the town green.

The train rolled on, speeding over Granite Junction and through the Alcott Tunnel, past Sherwood Die, where Oscar Williams and Todd Doggett hustled to beat the morning shift whistle. Next door, it looked like a big sale at the D&A, cars on display, washed, polished and shined.

Clanking, grinding, the twelve-car locomotive chugged along track and trestle traversing Main Street. Paperboys chucked the morning edition of the *Herald*, as neighborhood mongrels yipped playfully down the street behind bicycles with baseball cards in the spokes.

Inside Joe's, the gang was all there, stabbing stacks of pancakes, slurping strawberry shakes, carrying on about last night's big game, laughing and carefree. Girls danced to the latest rock 'n' roll blasting on the jukebox.

Then he saw her. Standing by the red payphone at the counter. Her back to him, long, straight raven hair still as black.

When he heard the phone ring, Ray felt as though the fabric of his skin would literally tear and fall from him and he'd just float far away; and the weight of fear shed from his shoulders and back like fifty-pounds of soaking flak.

There was never any doubt where he belonged. He'd just forgotten it for a moment.

She'd never leave him alone in this world.

ANOTHER MAN'S TREASURE

"He's just a skeezy old man that sells junk," Geiger says, sifting through scraps of aluminum foil in the dim candlelight, "what do you care?"

"I don't," I say.

"Then shut the fuck up."

It's just me and Geiger in the condemned church off 22nd and Mission. We've been squatting here for almost a year. Geiger used to sell meth to the decrepit priest who held the lease. The priest ain't around no more.

It's dark inside the church. No power. We got some butane candles in spread-out clumps, a mattress we dragged in from the street. Nobody bothered to turn off the water, so the toilet works. And you can't beat the rent.

"And who's that young boy he's always got with him?" Geiger asks, holding up and inspecting each piece of tin foil. "The dirty little fucker with the squinty eyes?"

"Donnie."

"Yeah, well, a dime bag says the old man's diddling Donnie. Which makes him a skeezy old man pervert, too." Geiger finds a scrap with a shiny golden nugget left, smiles, his loose, fishy mouth filled with decaying brown nubs. "You told him about the furniture, right?"

"I told him. But I don't want to hurt no one." Last week I asked the old man if he wanted to look at some furniture my mom is supposedly getting rid of.

"Christ," Geiger says, "you sound like a fucking after-school special."

Geiger sticks the broken pen straw in his mouth, puts fire to foil, sucks in a big hit. The flame illuminates a colorless face, revealing big sores and pusy scabs around sunken eyes, casting his distorted shadow like a racked ghoul against the broken-down altar. He exhales a thick silver cloud. There's nothing left of him except the yellow eyes, irises the size of nickels. "Stop being such a pussy and hit this."

He passes me the foil. I take to it like a starved rat to rotten alley fruit.

On Saturday, me and Geiger are back at the flea market down on Bayshore. It's early. The sun is up but you can't see it. A wall of fog has rolled off the ocean, heavy, wet, cold, blotting it out. It's usually foggy and cold this time of year but today is worse than usual. My hands are red and raw. I keep blowing on them. Despite the heavy ski coat I traded for a gram of speed, these winter winds chill to the bone.

Everyone's setting up shop. It's a pretty big deal, the flea market. It's where people like us—people without jobs—work, selling the merchandise they've salvaged from trash bins and junkyards. It's where Geiger and me make most of our money. Most of the vendors are tweakers too. They take meth to stay up all night and dumpster dive across the city while the rest of the world is asleep. You'd be amazed at what people throw out. High-tech electronics, stereos and speakers that only need a new plug or fuse, all easily fixable. Sometimes you can really score, like vintage train sets, or authentic army gear, even old-timey cigarette lighters like the kind my granddad used to have back in Kentucky. His was silver and shaped like a genie's lamp. He brought it home from the war. He always said it was a fair trade, since the Koreans took his leg. I took the lighter when I left Kentucky, sold it when I got here. I don't feel bad about too much of the stuff I done. I feel bad about that.

A lot of the vendors make what they sell—knitted hats and gloves, old hippies hocking dream catchers and pottery, original art. Geiger says it's all shit, but I think some of it's pretty cool. Like what the old man does. He collects dead cats, dogs and opossums, roadkill, then boils their heads, bleaching off the fur and turning the hides into bracelets, skull fragments into jewelry. The old man peddles other shit, too, like furniture and lamps, bed frames, mirrors carved all nice. But I like the jewelry best. Sometimes I help the old man and Donnie load up the trailer at the end of the day. The old man don't like Geiger. Once Geiger came around and tried to sell him shit, and the old man called him a parasite and hocked up a gob of snot. The old man might be the only seller here who doesn't do meth, even if he looks like he does, face all rubbery like one of those Halloween masks with the buggy eyes.

I like the old man. He reminds me of my granddad. A couple weeks back he gave me a bracelet and necklace. Didn't want no money for it or nothing. I got my fingers wrapped around the necklace now. I play with things when I get nervous.

"Stop daydreaming and pay attention," Geiger says to me. "I want to be sure he's got the same size roll of cash as last time."

We're walking around the flea market now, keeping an eye on the old man and Donnie. I don't like Donnie much. He looks inbred, all snaggletooth and crooked. You'd think he was twelve, he's so small, but when you get up close you can see he has whiskers. He's weird. Last Saturday when I was helping the old man, Donnie kept singing these little kid songs, nursery rhymes I remember my mom singing to me before she got killed, "London Bridge" and "Ring around the Rosy." Except when he was done, he'd say this fucked-up shit that ain't true. Like, "You know what 'London Bridge' is *really* about? It's about burying dead bodies." Or "'Ring around the Rosy' is about kids dying from the plague." Creepy ass shit. I never been able to figure out what his relationship with the old man is. Maybe Geiger's right and he's just the old man's bitch.

I still feel bad about what we're planning to do. But you can't argue with Geiger. For one, he's about ten years older, and about 50 lbs. heavier, and he's got a temper. I once seen him almost kill a man at this crumbly old house on the hill above the hospital. This junkie tried to get out of paying him, and Geiger started hitting him with a toaster he picked from the trash, damn near bashed his skull in.

We go seller to seller. All the fog makes it feel like we're walking through smoke on a battlefield. No one seems to be buying today. All we sell is a teenager, that's half an eight ball, and some lousy quarter bags. Which won't be nearly enough to re-up.

"It's OK," Geiger says.

Because we've seen the old man whip out his roll. And it's even bigger than last week.

It's later in the afternoon and everyone is packing up, loading the racks of clothes and TVs nobody bought, the power tools and mickey-moused lawn mowers and old framed Fillmore rock posters, into the backs of cluttered vans and trailers. It's a sad sight. Maybe Geiger's right and this is all nothing but a bunch of junk.

The fog drifts in thicker with the darkness.

"Do your thing," Geiger whispers.

I go help Donnie and the old man load the trailer. I ask the old man if he still wants to look at the furniture. Very much, he says, then stares over his shoulder at Geiger, who stands off in the distance.

"I don't know why you hang around with that trash," the old man says to me.

I shrug. Sometimes I don't know either.

I hoist the last box, slide it across the trailer's slick wood paneling. The inside of the trailer stinks like somebody died. You can see nasty red-brown stains from all the roadkill they scoop up. The old man slams the doors shut and hammers the padlock in place.

All I have to do now is get the old man to go inside an abandoned house on Potrero Hill for the furniture. Geiger says he'll take care of the rest. But I'm having second thoughts.

The three of us climb in the cab. The old man tells Donnie to give me a sandwich, which Donnie pulls from a brown sack on the floor.

"Looks like you could use something to eat," the old man says, kindly.

I nod. I am pretty hungry.

The old man passes me a bottle of soda. "Something to drink too."

My mouth is so dry, I chug the whole thing in one long gulp.

The streetlights look like fuzzy halos in the fog, all the zipping taillights on the overpass ahead, like tracers, racing between invisible stars...

It's the last thing I remember.

* * *

I come to with a terrific headache, my bones and muscles stretched and strained, like after pick-up football games in the winter back home in Kentucky. I try to open my eyes but they don't work so good, too crusted and swollen. Through a haze of orange light and swirling smoke, I can make out the outline of a hanging cow about to be butchered. Something tells me to avoid that light. Behind me, I feel a brighter light, a blinding vertical shaft, calling me. I want to move toward it but can't. I am an unattended puppet on a string. Finally the light bursts through and a bright sunshiny day comes into view. Only it ain't the day. It is the white-hot bulb from a clamped floodlight blazing in my eyes.

My eyes are all watery, like chemicals and dirt's been rubbed in them. I'm having a hard time breathing. My hands are over my head, ropes tied around my wrists. It feels like my shoulders are being ripped from the socket and I'm suffocating. All the pain comes now, one intense, searing flash, like a fire burns inside me, but on the outside my skin is cold.

I start to shiver so hard I almost spasm. It feels like I will break my own back. Now I understand why I am so cold. I don't have any clothes on.

Something groans beside me. I look over and see Geiger strung up and naked too, a side of beef hanging on a hook, his head slumped. I whisper his name but he don't answer. I can see where his skin's been pulled off his back and flank in long, neat strips, like straps of jerky to be dried.

"Geiger," I say again, but not too loud 'cause I don't want the old man or Donnie to hear me. But Geiger don't wake up. Whatever the old man drugged me with, he must've put twice as much into Geiger, 'cause I don't know how he's not screaming, all them red, bleeding nerves and blistery exposed muscles.

I wriggle my hands, but they ain't coming free. My heart is pounding so loud my ears are ringing. I gotta think. But I never been too good at that.

Someone fiddles outside with the padlock. I shut my eyes and pretend to be asleep.

"Open your eyes, boy," I hear the old man say with a huff and a groan as he climbs into the trailer. "I know damn well you're awake. I can hear you outside."

I open my eyes, and there's the old man dressed like a butcher, heavy canvas apron, rawhide gloves. He's holding a big tin bucket in one hand, a plastic jug in the other. Donnie stands beside him, rat-faced and smug.

Now Geiger screams. He's awake all right, feeling the pain of having been skinned alive. I wish I could cover my ears.

"You can stop that screaming," the old man says. "Ain't nobody can hear you."

Geiger rocks back and forth, snorting snot, which bubbles out his nose and mouth, dribbling down his quivering chin. Soon he gives up and starts whimpering. He reminds me of one of those coyotes we'd trap on the farm. You'd be sleeping in the house when a coyote would set off a trap. You hear coyotes in the wild baying all the time, but they don't sound like they do when they get trapped. In the wild, coyotes sound strong, confident, dangerous. When they're trapped, they stop howling and start acting docile, cowardly, because they're scared. They really will chew off their own paw if you let them. When you go out to finish them off, they don't bare their teeth or growl at you or nothing. They're meek as a house collie. I once seen a coyote lick my granddad's boot just like a pet dog. Before he put the shotgun between his eyes.

"Ain't so tough now, are you?" the old man says to Geiger. "I know what you were planning to do to me, try to take my money."

I look down at Donnie, who returns a devil's grin, and I know he must've followed us back to the church one night, eavesdropped as we made plans, the sneaky little weasel.

The old man reaches into the bucket, pulls out a hacksaw, which he passes to Donnie, and a box cutter. He slides the razor blade in and out, stepping in my direction.

"Please," I say. "I didn't do anything. It wasn't my idea."

With his bony hand, the old man shakes the box cutter at me. "But you was gonna do it just the same, weren't you? You wasn't gonna stop him. Makes you just as bad. Maybe even worse. 'Cause you know better."

The trailer doors are flung open out into the dark, black night. But there is nothing to see out there, just tall sea weeds blowing in the wind, the cold fog drifting around us like aimless ghosts cursed to wander the ends of the earth.

The old man stands in front of Geiger, who keeps blubbering.

"You think I'm just a crazy ol' coot who sells junk," the old man says.

"No, I don't," I say.

"It's OK," the old man says.

Donnie snickers.

"I *do* dabble in junk. And you and your friend here are the garbage."

The old man thrusts the box cutter into Geiger's stomach, sticks and sticks, yanks it up like he's gutting a steer, bloody entrails slopping to the floor. Geiger convulses in a seizure but doesn't die right away.

I try to break free, fight against the restraints. But it's useless.

The old man walks behind Geiger and slits his throat.

Donnie brings over a stool, steps on it and cuts Geiger down, his limp body flopping to the floor.

Donnie takes the jug the old man brought in, pours all its contents it into the bucket, turning his head to avoid the fumes, and even from where I hang, I can feel the toxic acid singeing my nose hairs. Donnie picks up the hacksaw, crouches beside Geiger and starts sawing away. First the fingers, then the hands, then the arms, the shoulder, and so on, dropping each part in the bucket, bleaching off the flesh.

And I understand now. The bloodstains on the floor. The leather bracelet on my wrist and bone necklace around my neck. None of it came from any roadkill.

The old man drags the stool in front of me, straddles it. "I come across garbage like you two all the time," the old man says, wiping the blood from the razor on his canvas apron. "In fact, I seek it out. I collect it. I take the scum and vermin, the refuse and waste no one else wants, and I make it useful again." He waggles the razor in front of me. "Because you know what they say. One man's trash…"

TRIPPING FOR BISCUITS

We'd assembled at the Terrapin Grill on Sunset Boulevard for an end-of-the-work-week celebration. The public relations firm I ran in those days had landed a high-profile client. By "high-profile," I mean about as big a starlet as there was going. Not that I'm the sort to go name-dropping. Then again, this isn't really about a famous Hollywood starlet, or even about me, for that matter. It's about a story told that late afternoon by a guy who'd been with us only a week, and from whom I haven't heard a word since. Normally, I wouldn't waste my time repeating a tall tale, but his story was so sensational, so outlandish—I'm sorry, but despite inherent skepticism, I have a hard time giving anybody the credit to make up something so fantastic.

There were four of us—me, Gwen, Lois, and the new guy, Douglas Reilly. In the short time he worked for me, Douglas displayed competence in his marketing research skills but otherwise wasn't terribly remarkable. Early thirties, thinning chestnut hair, doughy, the kind of man you pass a hundred times on the street and never look at twice. And unless it was job-related, he rarely spoke. When the girls asked him to join us, frankly I was shocked he agreed.

We'd ordered a bottle of pinot and an appetizer, parmesan-encrusted salmon patties with fried basil leaves, I think. I forget how the conversation started, but soon the girls had grown catty, gossiping about who had had what done, you know, various sordid tales of augmentation, collagen injections, breast implants, that sort of thing. Such conversation hardly interested me. I mean, who in Hollywood hasn't undergone a little nip and tuck?

They'd just finished dishing on an actress who'd had two inches of her backside removed ("But she's not even Latina!"), when one of the girls, Gwen or Lois, I forget which, asked Douglas to recount the weirdest plastic surgery case he'd encountered in the field.

Something about his countenance made us all stop what we were doing.

"I'm not sure it qualifies as 'plastic surgery,' per se," Douglas said, "but I did know this one guy." He looked so dreadfully intense, and I couldn't understand how a topic so mundane could elicit such a strong reaction. "He was a very good friend of mine, actually, and in the end..."

The waiter interrupted the mood by taking our dinner orders. When he left, Douglas collected himself and repeated this tale, which I have done my best here to reproduce, as close to verbatim as the human mind will allow. I, obviously, wasn't recording the conversation, but I've always prided myself on having remarkable recall. And, if nothing else, I can assure you, I've captured the sentiment.

Here is what he said:

"I met Jimmy Dugan senior year of high school, Hollings, Ohio, the town where I grew up. He transferred from the East Coast. Right away, you could tell Jimmy wasn't like other guys. For one, he was incredibly handsome. Beyond handsome, really, without a doubt, the finest looking man I've ever laid eyes on. Everyone, boys, girls, teachers, noticed it. And how a boy of seventeen could've sculpted that physique mystified me.

"The weird thing though, girls wanted nothing to do with him. Normally, a new boy in class, even one with moderately good looks, would've been the subject of incessant crushes. Not Jimmy.

"After a few weeks I remember talking to this girl in my science class, Alison Hodgson, a very pretty and popular student. I asked her why none of the girls fawned over the new kid. She said, 'It's his eyes. Something's not right there, like he's... from a different world.' When I asked her to elaborate, she couldn't, only adding that every girl she knew was terrified of him.

"Of course the guys weren't terrified of him. Still, no one seemed anxious to befriend him either.

"Jimmy and I had art class together that first semester, and in time, we began a casual acquaintance. His being so good looking and such a disaster with the ladies, I thought he might be, well, y'know.

"Back then, I looked much the same way I do now: nobody's prize but I never hurt for dates. Like most boys that age, my conversations tended to revolve around girls. So I tested the waters with Jimmy, throwing out names, and he certainly didn't respond like any homo. One day, I asked him, point blank. It was shortly before Homecoming Dance and I inquired whom he planned on taking. When he replied no one, I asked whether he even dug girls. Like I'd questioned whether he was bipedal or breathed air. '*Of course,* I like girls,' he said. Then after a moment, 'But girls don't like me.'

"Senior year rolled on, and Jimmy and I became good friends. And while he was certainly cordial with a number of other guys in school, I seemed to be the only close friend he had.

"Our friendship made sense, I suppose. We were both on the artsy side; neither of us played sports. And we shared something else in common: old movies. Though that hardly paints an accurate picture. What I mean to say, while I *liked* old movies—black and white detective pics, that sort of thing—Jimmy was *obsessed* with them. This obsession provided the first indication that Jimmy might be, well, slightly touched.

"An only child, Jimmy shared a tiny duplex with his mom. He never spoke of a father. Hollings was a nice town. Still is, but like any town, we had our less well-off sections, and Jimmy lived in one of those, by the turnpike, in the shadow of trucker motels, OTBs, and skin joints.

"His bedroom was in the attic, with barely enough space for a bed, television and VCR. The blistering pink neon sign from the Kit-Kat Club next door blazed so brightly into his room, I wondered how the poor guy got any sleep.

"Whenever there was a party, Jimmy passed. School function, dance, likewise. When I'd ask why, his reason was always the same: he'd recently gotten his hands on some old-time flick that he wanted to check out. Far as I could tell, that is all the kid did: watch film noir.

"Being a fan of the genre, I'd sometimes hang out and watch with him. It was quite an experience watching these movies with Jimmy. After Alison's comments, I took to studying his eyes, which were, to tell the truth, otherworldly. An impossibly bright cobalt blue, they were strangely...lifeless. This all changed, however, when Jimmy was in front of his television. There, as though a switch had been tripped, they'd come alive, the blue of his irises literally illumined.

"He knew everything about every actor. And *even more* about the actresses. Martha Vickers, Mary Astor, Ann Savage, Alida Valli. Like some guys chart Playboy Pets, Jimmy kept a running log of these gals' hobbies. What their favorite meal was, what size shoe they wore, their best childhood memory. He had notebooks filled with that stuff. And whenever one of these ladies graced the screen, he'd gaze forlorn, as if he were actually in love with her."

"Douglas," I interrupted, ripping a hunk of table bread, "plenty of people like old movies or other odd things. I don't see why this should strike you as so bizarre."

Douglas took a sip of wine. "I am looking back, of course, knowing things that I haven't told you yet." He held up a hand. "Let me finish.

"After graduation, I went off to Columbia, and Jimmy and I stayed in touch via the sporadic letter or occasional phone call. But soon those correspondences waned. And, one day, he disappeared."

"Disappeared?"

"I called his mother's house and that's what she said. No note. Not even a phone call. He'd simply packed his things and moved out, and she hadn't heard from him in over a year."

"You were his friend," I said. "He never mentioned any plans to you?"

"He didn't go to college?" Lois asked.

Douglas took the napkin off his lap, face turning red. "No, he did not go to college. And he never went on dates with girls. It was those goddamned pictures!"

Exhaling heavily, Douglas recomposed himself. "I'm afraid, I haven't told the story properly. When I say Jimmy was entranced by old films, I can't do that infatuation justice. It's all he talked about. All he cared about. It's *all* he ever did. Which is why, when I finally did hear from him again, his news, while of course startling, wasn't as difficult to wrap my brain around as perhaps it should have been."

"What happened?"

"A few years back, having not heard from Jimmy in all that time, I received a late night phone call. I had moved several times since our last contact, both in and out of state, and how he'd been able to track me down was a mystery. My parents had passed a few years earlier. So that was my first question: How on earth did you find me? He said that was his job these days. He was a PI."

"A private investigator?" I said, incredulously. "Sounds like some—"

"Old movie," Douglas quickly retorted. "Exactly.

"He said he had recently moved to Southern California to open his practice, the Jimmy Dugan Private Investigation Agency.

"Our conversation that night was short, but we made arrangements to meet for lunch the following afternoon.

"I arrived early at Citrix off Santa Monica and secured a table outside. I wondered if I'd still be able to recognize my friend. I, after all"—Douglas pointed to the top of his crown—"had lost a little up top, put on a couple pounds, as men our age are wont to do. Such concern was for naught. I spotted him immediately; he didn't look a day older. But his attire! Gray suit, with dark gray shirt, tie, and a display handkerchief, black brogues—in short, exactly like Humphrey Bogart in *The Big Sleep*.

"'Hi'ya, kid,' he said to me, with a broad grin and slap on the back.

"Jimmy sat down and pulled out a monogrammed, silver cigarette case from his breast pocket, and with a precision I've only seen onscreen tapped an unfiltered off the table, flipped it in the air and caught it in his lips, lighting a match off his thumbnail, a very smooth gesture, indeed.

"To see someone in modern day Hollywood, dressed like that, carrying on with those mannerisms, you can imagine how strange it looked. But Jimmy didn't display a hint of self-consciousness. When we were younger, his sensitivity toward other's perception of him betrayed an extremely insecure man. This current incarnation came across as anything but.

"We ordered. Actually, I was the only one eating, Jimmy opting for the liquid lunch: double scotch, straight up. He drank several throughout the course of the meal, though he never appeared drunk.

"He asked what I'd been up to, and I filled him in, how I'd graduated with a degree in public relations but had had a tough time finding work back east, thus prompting my decision to move west. Pleasantries.

"It was a typical sunny SoCal day. The sidewalks teemed with a mix of cosmopolitan and bohemian, beautiful people in the latest mannequin fashions, beach bums with puka shell necklaces and cut-off jeans, loud colors and louder conversations, but it was Jimmy, in his dull gray suit and fedora, framed by the tiny wild orange trees lining the boulevard, who shone the brightest that afternoon.

"I inquired, What about him? Besides the recently opened practice, what had he been doing all this time? And it was then he told me about his life-changing decision."

Douglas drizzled a pool of olive oil onto his plate and dabbed some bread crust.

"Well?" the girls implored in unison.

Douglas smirked, the proverbial cat with his canary. "Jimmy's father, it turns out, had been a wealthy man, something Jimmy failed to mention during our time together, and apparently he too was not without his peculiarities. When he passed, the old man didn't leave the mother a cent, instead putting it all in a trust for his only son.

"When Jimmy turned twenty-one, he suddenly found himself very rich. After I left, he said he didn't have a friend in town, and with all that money he didn't see any reason to stay.

"Stashing some feed for his mom, he packed his bags and dusted out of dodge. For the next several years, Jimmy kicked around the country, working odd jobs in various border towns, playing butter and egg man for the ladies. He'd hoped maybe geography would provide a cure. But wherever he went, Jimmy encountered the same strange looks and feelings of alienation. Nothing had changed. He was still an outcast.

"Jimmy said it got so bad, he starting thinking of doing the unthinkable. The only thing that stopped him was the possibility of an afterworld devoid of his one, true passion: old film noir pictures. And with that thought, he said, suddenly, everything became clear.

"It wasn't this world; it was this *time*, this modern age. Of course, all the money in the world can't buy a time machine. So Jimmy said he did the next best thing."

Douglas raised his hands, palms upward, as though he were about to perform a magic trick for twelve-year-olds, pausing for dramatic effect. He leaned across the table and whispered, "He had the color removed from his vision—so that he would see the world only in black and white." He wiped his hands clean.

The girls and I exchanged curious looks, before I began laughing. "Good one, Douglas. You almost had me. That simply isn't possible."

"I didn't believe so, either," Douglas continued, undeterred. "But Jimmy did not back down from his claim. He said it took a long time to find a doctor willing to perform the procedure, and that, ultimately, it cost him virtually all his inheritance."

"C'mon," Lois said, "how does someone get the color removed from his eyes?"

"Not from *his eyes*," Douglas calmly stated. "From *his vision*. The eyes retained their otherworldly blue brilliance. And I don't know, to answer your specific question, how the operation worked. But apparently it isn't impossible. Jimmy gave me a rudimentary lesson. Basically, our eyes break down into two components: rods and cones. The former handles light, blacks and whites, the latter color. Jimmy merely had his cones disengaged somehow."

"I'm still not sure I'm buying this," Gwen said.

"And neither did I. *At first*. I concluded my friend had suffered a psychotic break and there was nothing I could do for him. For the rest of our luncheon, I smiled a lot, and planned on never seeing the crazy bastard again.

"But now that we lived in the same city, of course I did see him again. And I began to realize that whether or not the surgery actually took place was irrelevant. Because, *in his mind*, he firmly believed it had. And his claim, however preposterous, was not without supporting evidence.

"The first time I went to his office, I had to walk through the slums, bowery bums passed out, crack fiends, dope dealers on the corner, whores crawling from back seats, the whole nine yards. Spring and 5th is a very sordid intersection. Decaying, degenerate America smacked rudely with every breath of exhaust and ether. But once I climbed those three flights and pushed through the heavy mahogany doors, it was like I'd been transported to another world.

"Inside was an exact replica of Sam Spade's office in *The Maltese Falcon*, down to the smallest detail, which included the secretary, who was the spitting image of Lee Patrick, same uptight blonde bob, same conservative black pant suit, same terse grin. I almost asked if the hire had been contingent upon remaining in character. She instructed me to 'wait in the sitting room while she rang Mr. Dugan.'

"When I get buzzed into his office, there's Jimmy, doing his best Philip Marlowe, feet on the desk, half a bottle of corn camped by his feet, cigarette dangling from his lips, shuffling a deck of nudie playing cards.

"He said something like, 'Sorry for the delay, goose. Just got off the phone with the DA's boys downtown. Had to tighten the screws after tooting the wrong ringer. Somebody's got to step off for this caper.'

"And that's the way he always talked now. One needed a hard-boiled glossary to even understand him. 'Horses' were 'bangtails,' 'money' was 'cabbage,' 'guns,' 'roscoes' or 'gats.' It was unreal. Yet, being around him was so strangely fascinating. I kept thinking back to what he said, about not being able to invent a time machine and having to do the next best thing. I'm here to tell you, whatever you may or may not believe, Jimmy Dugan found a way to trump the space/time continuum. He now existed entirely within that realm of yesteryear film noir. He talked the talk, he walked the walk. The hard drinking, hard fighting low life of the shamus. And remember how I said that Jimmy, despite his movie star good looks, couldn't attract a female? Well, the fighting and drinking soon started taking their toll, and that pretty face took one helluva beating, but the uglier he grew, the better looking his girls—or 'dames' as he called them—got."

"Over the next couple years, I saw quite a bit of Jimmy. I had to. Away from him, the remote of my life remained stuck on pause, a safe but boring vacuum. But with Jimmy—I was a bona fide co-star, smack dab in the middle of the glamorous 1940s. I'd schlep through my dull day, and then trade glossy high-rise for dingy skid row, where Jimmy'd fill me in on his latest case or whatever femme fatale was driving him wild with passion that week. And, damned, if I wasn't getting sucked up into it, too.

"Soon, I started going with him on stakeouts. He'd fit me with a gat, and I had to be ready to use it. Who knew Tinseltown crawled with so many nymphomaniac heiresses hell-bent on revenge, so many ex-prize fighters desperately seeking a last shot at redemption? Sometimes things got hairy. I learned to handle myself with my mitts." Douglas showed us his hands. They trembled. "But I suppose it's good things ended the way they did, for me at least. A man can't live with that sort of duality for long."

Douglas shook his head. "Never met anyone else like him."

Our food arrived and Douglas began spicing his plate, while we all anxiously waited for him to resume, mouths agape.

"What happened to him?" I finally asked.

"In short?" Douglas said, shoveling a forkful of mutton. "Got fitted with the Chicago overcoat. Some high roller's doll put him on the nut, and he began owing shylocks serious lettuce. He tried to push orphan paper to escape the droppers, but with all that booze souping the kidneys, his grifts were as useful as a bindle stiff." Douglas chuckled with a snort. "They found him with two slugs in his belly at the bottom of the Lido pier, still wearing his shades. Would you believe those coppers ruled it a suicide? Talk about a trip for biscuits."

That was our lunch, and that was his story. He didn't say another word about it, no matter how much we pressed. That was Friday. Monday rolled around and Douglas Reilly didn't show up for work. For some reason, I wasn't surprised. I tried reaching him on his cell but found it disconnected.

As for his story, as time goes on I remain unconvinced. I've been around long enough to know some folks crave attention so desperately they'll say just about anything. New guy on the job, wants to make an impression... My cousin's an eye doctor, and after Douglas's disappearance I phoned him and recounted this tale, asking if such a thing were even possible. Of course he said no.

It wasn't long after that I grew tired of the public relations game, all those phonies with their plastic body parts. I sold my interests to a junior partner and moved down to San Diego. I bought a little bungalow on the beach, where I write this now.

I often think about Douglas Reilly and his crazy story. I don't know why it still resonates as strongly as it does, why, after all these years, I can vividly recall the way that mousy man's dull eyes came to life while telling it.

Really, have you ever heard of such a thing?

THE BURNOUT

This was supposed to happen to older cops, not guys my age—and especially not to wunderkinds who'd made history as the youngest to detective. Maybe that was the problem. I'd been so focused for so long, climbing through ranks, distinguishing myself from the competition, that I'd squeezed an entire career into a handful of years, and with it drained the life from the very thing I loved. Maybe I was over-thinking it. Either way, there I stood, barely thirty-five and suffering the big burn out. So I'd handed in my resignation and had only one week left on the job.

Then I met her.

Moving up that ladder, I stepped over a lot of folks and hurt a lot of feelings. Which is why I got the call to investigate a two-bit heist on Sixth Street, home to the city's most undesirable: pimps, whores, junkies, your basic riff-raff, all corralled in a degenerate square nicknamed Crack Central.

I spotted Soyka standing by the door. I poked my head inside to see an old Jewish man bleeding from his.

"What happened?" I asked, digging a cigarette from my coat pocket.

"Botched smash and grab. Couple crackheads. They didn't get anything."

I gave Soyka the once-over, the disinterested expression and sagging middle-aged paunch, so indicative of the beat-down, seasoned veteran. There's nothing worse than that cop who's stopped believing in what he's fighting for.

"Hit him over the head? With what?"

"An iron," he grumbled.

"An iron?"

"That's what the man says. An iron."

Goddamn crackheads. Attempt a hold-up and the best weapon they can find is an iron.

Then it struck Soyka that this job hardly required my presence. "What the hell they send you for?"

"Guess they don't want this last week made easy."

"That's right, you're leaving us."

Us? Like we worked at Sears-Roebuck together, unloading tractor trailers and sharing a beer before heading to separate suburban homes to surf Internet porn.

"The old man talking?" I asked.

"Couple skinny black kids, all he says."

I gazed toward Market Street and the tourists only a couple blocks away, watched as they headed to Union Square to take a goddamn trolley ride, swinging bags of designer merchandise, capturing staged joy and paying no heed to the wretchedness just a few feet south.

"Anybody see anything?" I asked, already knowing the answer. These types protect their own.

Soyka gestured with a lazy backhand. "Got a girl up there. Caught her doing business in a parked car, may've gotten a look." A wry smile crept over his face. "Actually, you should take a look at this one."

"That bad?"

"Just the opposite. Tell you what, if they made them like that, maybe I wouldn't mind this job so fucking much." He spat a gob of yellow, which affixed to the sidewalk like rubber cement, jiggling.

She sat on the hood of a cruiser. Couldn't have been older than nineteen, twenty but Soyka wasn't lying. Sixth Street whores don't normally come built like that. Wavy chestnut hair and porcelain complexion. What a doll.

I squashed my cigarette.

"Got an extra one of those, honey?"

Most girls can't pull off a "honey" like that. She could. I passed her my pack.

I tried to remain professional, extracting the small notepad from my inner pocket, flipping pages with a quick thumb-lick, eyes peeled to the ground. "I hear you got a look at the boys who did this."

"I know them," she said.

"You know them?"

"Not *know-know*, but y'know." She paused, casually looking away.

I got it. "But you're not talking, that it? Or maybe you want to wait until the next time you're picked up—"

She giggled. "One of them goes by Ricky Two Flats. The other they just call T. I think they run for the Vietnamese owner around the corner."

I didn't write a word.

Then, like a cheerleader leaving a pep rally, she hopped off the hood, confident and unabashed. She grazed my arm, gazing up with those big brown peepers. "Can I go now, officer?"

* * *

The name she gave was Becky Marshall, which even sounded like a cheerleader's name. Next night, I found myself trolling Sixth Street. The crackheads had been picked up and charged, so I wasn't looking for them.

It felt strange, heart thumping madly in my chest, because I soon realized what it was: I'd developed a crush. A crush on a whore.

I pulled in front of a liquor store to grab some smokes. It had been a long time since I'd had a romantic relationship. Being a detective doesn't leave much time for that sort of thing. But a man needs to have an object of affection every once in a while, needs to send flowers and be able to say tender things. He needs that as much as he needs the other stuff.

I paid for the pack, goofy grin on my face, pleased that I'd deduced the silly reason behind irrational feelings.

"Looks like somebody's having a good time."

I turned and there she stood, a Midwestern farmer's daughter just off the hayride. I stammered a greeting of sorts, but tongue-tied I must've sounded like an idiot. I hurried out the door.

She followed me out. "What's the rush?"

"I have a job—" I said, spinning around, and that's when I saw her left eye, which had been shielded inside the store. It was badly bruised, the color of uncooked, pummeled beef.

I took her by the shoulders. "My God, what happened?"

"I don't even know your name."

"Eddie," I said. "Eddie Cage."

"Detective Eddie Cage," she repeated sadly. "Where's your car?"

I steered us over California trolley tracks, past the behemoth five-star hotels and into the mansion neighborhoods overlooking the sea of Pacific Heights, the million dollar homes where I'd never live.

"Are you going to tell me what happened?" I asked.

"You know how the game works."

Yeah, I knew how the game worked. Two sides of the same coin that game.

I fired up a cigarette and offered her one, which she gratefully took.

"Surely, a girl your age must have other options."

"I'm not as young as you think," Becky said. "You know a girl like me can't just walk away. There's other people involved."

"Who? Your pimp? No sale, darling; you just walk away. What can he do?"

She turned slowly. "This," she said pointing to her eye.

I reached for the CB.

"What are you doing?"

"Sending someone to pick his ass up."

"And he'll be out in a couple hours."

She was right, of course. I'd made similar collars a hundred times. Ink's not even dry before they're back on the street.

I paused atop the Heights, overlooking the whole of the city spread below. The crumbling tenements of broken dreams. So much suffering. So many sick fucks looking for a way to cash in on another's pain. I wanted to punch my fist through a wall.

I pulled my gun and laid it on the dash.

"He isn't worth it, Eddie," she said. "I'm not worth it."

"He might not be. But *you* are."

She twisted her small body and grabbed my face. She kissed me hard. It was as perfect and pure a kiss as I'd ever felt.

I took her home with me that night, and we stayed up talking through dawn. She told me her sad story, how she'd come to this cold place, leaving behind Lawrence, Kansas, at fifteen to escape the fumbling hands of her stepfather, her mother long deposited in the local sanitarium. Her sister wasn't so fortunate. I'd heard a lot of stories during my time on the force, but none that so tugged at my unflappable sense of honor and decency, the very fabric of right and wrong. How she wound up in the clutches of this D. White Love character, which was the name of the man who owned her body and soul, was no less a twisted, perverted and evil tale.

Over the next few days, I saw Becky as often as I could. As the week came to an end, I'd gotten her to agree to come away with me. We'd hit 101 and never look back.

But Thursday evening threw a wrench in those plans.

Sitting at the precinct, wrapping up paperwork, I got the call, and raced in my car to the corner of Sixth.

Mascara ran down those pretty cheeks, splattered blotches over a cold-cocked chin.

Back at my place, I had her lie down on the couch, while I went to the kitchen for an ice pack.

"I had to tell him about us. He went crazy!"

I told her not to talk and to ice her swollen jaw.

"We're gonna leave this awful place, aren't we, Eddie?"

"Soon as I can arrange for the furniture and things, yes."

"How long will that take?!" Becky screamed. She started rocking, the way troubled girls do.

"Calm down."

"He said he'll *kill me*! He will! You don't know him. I've seen him do it before."

"Hold on, Becky. You've actually seen this D. White murder? That's a serious accusation."

She bolted upright, pointing wildly at her smashed-up mouth. "And this isn't!" She threw the ice pack across the room. "Maybe you're not who I thought you were, Eddie."

She made for the door. I grabbed her arm.

She tore away. "You're still a cop. Even if your paychecks stop tomorrow, you're still a cop. You see my battered face, and it's, 'Sit down, relax,' but, oh, there might be a murder investigation, and Eddie's off to save the day."

"That's not fair."

"Nothing's fair! Is it fair the way fat, old men have violated me, humiliated me?"

"I told you the other night that I'd have him arrested."

"*Arrested?* What kind of *a man* are you, Eddie? A guy beats up the woman who loves you, and you want to do it by the book?"

"What did you say?" I asked softly.

"A guy beats up the woman who loves you." Her eyes retreated from smoldering to kitten. She looked up at me like I was the strongest man in the world. "I do, Eddie. I do. With all my heart."

During my time on the force, I'd performed my services honorably, respecting my fellow cops and treating every prisoner courteously. And what did it get me? My fellow cops despised me, and those same criminals I'd treated with such respect? Most were back in business, slipping through various liberal loopholes. The real question was, What had I done for the overall welfare of the city? The answer? Not a goddamn thing.

Tucking Becky in, I accepted my unique position. Finally, I could bypass protocol and use my authority towards a good end. Judge, jury, executioner.

And the money she told me about? Hell, I knew what they did with money seized in such cases. It'd get locked in an evidence room, left to be picked clean by a different breed of vulture. No, this money was Becky's severance pay, and the poor girl deserved that much.

I had my story. I heard screaming, walked in through an unlocked door to investigate. The man shot, I shot back. A detective with my credentials, no one would question a thing.

I parked in a Crack Central alley. Creeping up the stairs over scattered shoes and dead mice, I pulled my gun and used the key she'd given me.

D. White was alone, like Becky had said he would be, dozed off in front of a soundless television, which slapped dark waves off scarred walls.

Late forties, maybe early fifties, the toll of a lifestyle exacting its pointed revenge. He slouched in his La-Z-Boy, face covered with the day's growth. Bottle of booze camped between his legs, he looked defeated. For a man who wreaked so much havoc, he didn't look like much to me.

I didn't relish shooting a sleeping man. Fortunately, I didn't have to. Love opened his eyes. Instead of fear, I saw silent resignation. The guilty always know they've got it coming.

D. White Love rubbed his chin. "Can I help you, friend?" he said, voice thick with sleep and alcohol.

"I'm a friend of Becky's."

He chortled.

"You find this funny?"

"Sure. Little tart sends one of her boyfriends to collect her blood money. That's funny stuff, brother."

"You got some nerve talking about her like that."

He leaned forward, catching my eye. "I see the little whore has gotten to you, too."

I shot him between the eyes.

The money was right where Becky said it would be. Quite the pile. I planted the gun in D. White's lifeless hands and fired two shots into the wall.

Outside on Tahoma, while the foot patrol finished up the busywork inside, I lit a cigarette, drawing on the stiff scent of satisfaction.

Last day on the job, I'd finally done the right thing. And it felt goddamn good.

My mind drifted to what would happen next, the hero's welcome and reward, the two of us in a quaint cottage somewhere in the northern hills. Maybe we could use the bread to open a little bed and breakfast, where well-mannered guests would stop by to enjoy a civilized weekend far from the hectic grind of the metropolis. I grew tickled thinking what my life would be like until my dying days.

Soon I saw Soyka dragging his slug-like body down the alley, pulling up beside me.

"Helluva last night, Cage."

Up the block, the coroner's boys hauled the black-cloaked gurney, loading it into the back of a van.

"You know these Sixth Street types," I said, "always quick with the trigger."

"It'll be interesting to see what drugs they find in his system."

"I don't know about drugs," I said. "But he was definitely drunk."

"Booze? You kidding me? Must be PCP. Crack isn't even enough. Ketomene, maybe. What else could cause a man like that to take a pot shot at a cop?"

I flicked my butt to the ground. "Who knows why these pimps do anything they do?"

A peculiar expression came over his doughy face. "Pimp? What makes you think the guy was a pimp?"

I replayed everything I knew. But I realized all I knew was what Becky had told me.

"You know what I mean," I said. "Players. Pimps. Whatever they're calling themselves these days."

Soyka relaxed. "Sure. But I'm not sure ol' Dwight Lovitz ran with that sort of crowd. Really, what would make a second shift foreman at a print shop get so jumpy? Mutherfucker didn't have so much as a speeding ticket on file. Anyway, I'm sending a prowl car to pick up his girlfriend."

"His girlfriend?"

"Yeah. Actually, it's that girl from the other night? Remember, at the Jew's shop, the piece of ass giving head for fifty bucks?"

"You just said Lovitz worked at a print shop."

Soyka crinkled his nose. "Pimp? Oh, now I get it. You filed the fucking report. Christ, I can be thick. No, the girl's not a whore. Well, actually, I guess she is, if she's trading sex for money. But not *that kind* of whore. From what I hear she's just got a bad case of the hotpants. You know, the itch? More a slut with an entrepreneurial side. No real money in it like that. I mean, can you imagine how many cocks a girl would have to suck to stockpile anything significant? Makes you feel almost sorry for the poor bastard you shot, don't it? Poor fucker's off, busting his tail while she's selling hers. Well, I suppose a piece of ass like that can make a sucker out of a lot of men." He laughed loudly, fat pie hole stretching to showcase yellow teeth and quivering blubber tongue.

I watched through steam rising as the ambulance pulled away and police switched on their sirens to hunt another bad man. Screams and curses rained down around me, seeming to come from all directions, windows, doors, fire escapes, rooftops, the nighttime lullaby of the cityscape. And I knew then that I could never leave this place. I was tied to her forever.

A MATTER OF TRUST

"Drive!" I scream and drop the bag, reaching across my battered, bleeding body to slam the door shut. My right arm dangles at my side, useless.

"Where?" she asks.

"Just drive. And take it easy. These roads are icy deathtraps. I don't want to end up in a ditch."

I try to brush the snow and ice from my hair but I'm having a hard time moving or breathing, and wince with every motion. I'm pretty sure I broke some ribs when I slid down the embankment and flopped on the drainpipe. But at least the bullet went through. I think. I bonked my head pretty good. My brain feels like a blender on frappe.

I don't know how I even managed to stand, or stumble into the middle of the old access road on two feet, let alone aim my gun into the only pair of headlights in the middle of a goddamn blizzard. And considering the motel where we'd been holed up, the Candlelight, is in the sticks, it's a goddamn miracle anyone was out this time of night at all.

But I think I'll hold off thanking God just yet.

"I'm not sure where you want me to drive—"

"Listen, sweetheart, I'll let you know when to turn, OK?" I give her the once over. It's hard to see in the dark. She's got something covering her head but a blonde tendril curls out. She looks put together, everything where it should be, pert little nose, full ruby lips. Something about her feels vaguely familiar, probably because I grew up around here and the women are all the same.

I should tell her that if she does what I say, she'll be OK, but I don't particularly care about pleasantries right now. My brother is missing. The kid is dead. I've been shot and the cops are after me.

How did it all turn to such shit?

* * *

I didn't like the job from the start. Too many wrinkles outside the norm. The reason I'd been successful this long is never straying from what works. My brother Ash and I had been in this business since we were kids, from liquor stores to armored cars; and while other guys were doing long stretches, neither of us had so much as seen a jail cell overnight. And it hadn't been a matter of luck.

The first problem was the job itself. Ash and I had rules we lived by, one of the biggest being never work close to home. This job was practically in our backyard.

The pros have two tiers, the folks who arrange the job, and the ones who pull it off. Peter Prince did the arranging, and Ash and I did the stealing. A hairy beast of man who hailed from the islands, Prince always smelled like sugar and cinnamon. But he was rock solid as they come. He said if we wanted to ball this time, we'd have to play on our home court.

The game this time was stones. Usually diamonds were too much of a headache to even bother. Security systems, armed escorts, a royal pain in the ass. Not like the old days, when a couple salesmen transported them in trays in the trunk. It was a simpler time then. But Prince had gotten a line on a couple boys doing it old school.

Word was Edmund Herschlin was getting out of the business, too old to give a fuck about joining the high-tech parade. Ol' Ed was the biggest independent jeweler in the North and he'd be liquidating the remainder of his wares in our neck of the woods. Most of his boys, old farts left over from the Truman administration, rarely carried guns, and if they did, they wouldn't know how to fire the damn things.

Ash and I were coming off a shaky job over in Chicago, payroll deposit on the Gray Line, probably the closest we'd come to getting caught. In fact, when Ash hadn't shown at the rendezvous, I was certain our streak was over. Or at least his was. I should've known better than to doubt him.

But it scared me. It's a criminal cliché, I know, one last job, but after Chicago, I really was thinking of hanging it up.

Then this puppy fell in our lap. Ash convinced me, if I were serious about quitting, to take the easy money. Hard to argue. I wouldn't be getting a 9-to-5 anytime soon.

Except that when it looks too good to be true, it usually is. And it's never just a matter of money.

*　*　*

The winter wind lashes, wobbling the tin sign that reads Old State Road 23. Or maybe it's my brain that's wobbling. It's all coming down now, snow, sleet, ice, the heavens pitching a violent fit. With the weather, she takes it nice and slow. Just how I like it. I keep my eyes peeled, front and back. No cars, either direction.

"Expecting someone?" she asks.

"Just drive." I kick the medicine bag with the stones at my feet, pull the cigarettes from my inside pocket with my good arm, slide one up. I jab in the dash's lighter. My right side throbs. I'm pretty sure it went through. So why won't it stop bleeding?

The lighter pops. She reaches over. "Here, let me." She holds the cherry tip steady as I lean forward to take a big inhale.

These tiny towns spread out up here, but I know Rochester can't be more than forty, fifty miles straight ahead. There, I can make some calls, find out what the fuck happened. But in this weather, who knows how long that's going to take, and I'm not feeling so hot.

Then the pain hits, a prolonged wave I can feel through every nerve and cell, all the way to the back of my teeth, which begin to chatter, before involuntarily clamping down.

"What am I supposed to do if you die in my car?"

I try to sit up, grinding my molars. "I'm not going to die. A bullet went in and out. I'm going to be fine. Now you do what I tell you, you'll be fine, too."

"I'm not a nurse, but—" Icy rain continues thrumming the windshield and roof, so hard it sounds like a hail of ammunition "—maybe we should pull off."

"Where do you think we can pull off, lady? We're in the middle of goddamn blizzard, in the middle of goddamn nowhere. There's a roadside motel back up that hill where you picked me up. And if you think we're going back there, you're nuts. Just drive." I pause. I'm feeling funny, starting to get a little paranoid.

I bring the gun to her temple. "Why are you even out on a night like this?"

She keeps her cool, eyes locked on the road. "I'm leaving my husband, if you must know."

I lower the gun. "Well, you might've picked a better night. Not that I don't appreciate the ride."

"The night sort of picked me, if you know what I mean."

Yeah, I guess I do.

She reaches into the center console and pulls out a bottle of water. "At least drink this."

I twist the cap off with my teeth. Take a slug, then rinse the blood from my mouth and pour it on my wound.

"Sorry about your car," I say.

She smiles. "Don't worry about it. It belongs to my husband."

* * *

Being right in our backyard bothered me. How neat it all seemed bothered me. Usually either one of those things should've been enough for me to pull out.

Then Prince made a last minute addition. Said we needed a wheelman, just in case, and that he had the perfect guy.

The kid's name was Danny Bunyan. Neither Ash nor I had ever heard of him, and we got in a big fight over it.

"How long we known Prince?" Ash said.

He didn't need me to answer.

"Prince says your good people, you're good people."

Ash was right. I owed it to him to at least meet the kid.

The meet and greet was set up at Waylon's, a truck stop in Zumbrota. We were told this Danny was young and that he would be wearing a blue ball cap. He was wearing a blue ball cap, all right. And he was young. Really young.

We had beers, talked particulars. Right away Danny put me at ease. He talked a good game. Mostly, he'd worked as a wheelman, but he'd been a bagman plenty. He told some stories. I listened for holes in his stories, for anything out of place, but my bullshit meter didn't twitch. And the longer we sat in the roadside, the more I started liking the kid. He reminded me of me when I was starting out.

A car horn beeped, and I tensed.

"Relax," Danny said, "That's just my sister."

"What the fuck?"

"My brother's right," Ash said. "You can't have your sister coming around."

"She's just picking me up. She thinks I'm filling out an application to tend bar. I'm not stupid, guys."

I was just starting to relax, when he took off his ball cap.

Flaming red hair.

You make your living perfecting your craft, developing technique and approaching everything with a cold, critical eye. But you still need to trust your gut, and you don't fuck with superstition. Everyone knows: red hair is bad juju.

We watched as Danny got in the car with his sister, who best I could tell was a redhead, too. Terrific. A family of goddamn redheads.

* * *

"You're bleeding badly," the woman says. "You need a hospital."

"Just drive," I repeat, although I'm not sure that's what comes out, the words sort of slithering, slurring. My brain feels like it's bobbing on a bog of molasses, the rest of me being pulled down. I look over at her, try to focus. Her face is changing color, sharp shadows dancing like devils on a grave in the moonlight...

* * *

Everything had started out fine. We caught up with the diamond men around midnight, just past Riesling at a desolate rest stop, a swoop and grab. Danny was as skilled a wheelman as Prince had said he would be, pinning them in their car while Ash and I hopped out and took care of the rest. The salesmen were about a hundred years old, and they gave up the trays, no problem. They crawled into the trunk like little boys going down for an overdue nap.

As Ash and I started to get in the car, Danny got out.

"What are you doing?" I said. "Get back inside."

"We can't leave their car here," Danny said.

"What are you talking about?"

"I just saw a truck up on the highway flip a bitch and make for this exit."

"So what?" Ash said.

"I didn't see any truck. Ash?"

"I wasn't looking at the highway."

"We don't have time," Danny said. "Trust me. We've got to move—now." He handed me the keys. "You drive. I'll get rid of the car, get a hold of you at the Candlelight."

"Fuck that," Ash said.

"You're holding the diamonds," Danny said. "What's the problem?"

"That's not how we do it," I said.

"I don't know how you two *do it*," said Danny, "but I'm telling you, I saw a truck up there get off this exit—"

"Who gives a shit?" Ash said. "Maybe they forgot milk at the store—"

"What store? We're in the middle of fucksake nowhere—"

I reached inside the salesman's car, yanked the key from the ignition, a single one on a giant ring with a diamond-encrusted logo and the words Let It Shine. I passed the key to my brother. "I'll go with Danny to the Candlelight. You head south, leave the car at Lyman's." Lyman's was the old junkyard off 73. It's where we left a lot of things we didn't want being found for a while. "Call Prince when you get there. Get a hold of us at the motel."

* * *

We'd been at the Candlelight for over three hours. No Ash. Prince wasn't picking up either. And out of nowhere, a brutal winter storm had rolled in.

A freak blizzard. A goddamn redhead. It's not a matter of signs. You know when the chips are stacked against you.

I was taking a piss when I heard the sirens coming up the drive. I grabbed the bag, bolting for the back door. "Let's go!"

But that redheaded bastard just sat there on the bed, looking at me like a lost puppy dog.

I wasn't waiting. I pulled my gun and ran. I heard the front door kicked down, the shots whizzing by, and craned my neck to catch the kid flopped facedown on the floor.

I ran through the dense snowy woods, and one good thing about the storm, if they were behind me, they couldn't see shit.

On the ledge overlooking the road, I grabbed a branch to navigate down the icy embankment. I felt a stinging beneath my ribs. I looked down and saw the blood. Then the branch broke and I fell down the hill.

* * *

"You don't look so good," she says.

I'll be OK. Don't worry about me, I say, holding up the gun, only I realize I'm not holding up the gun. It lies there, limp in my lap. And no words are coming out of my mouth, either. I'm paralyzed.

She reaches over and grabs the gun, peeling it effortlessly from my flaccid fingers, then gently steers off the road, where she pets my head like I'm a stupid dog. I can't move a muscle, can't even blink.

A car approaches from the other direction, slowing down, and pulling in front of us. And as its headlights spread, I see the peroxide box on the floor, the giant key ring with the diamond-encrusted logo dangling in the ignition. I think I detect the faint scent of cinnamon.

She reaches over, grabs the bag at my feet, lifts the pack of cigarettes off my lap, fires two up, and sticks one in my mouth. She laughs when it falls right back out.

"I know what you're asking yourself," she says. "Who was it? Danny? Your brother? Prince? Maybe all of them?" She lifts my head, squares it out the windshield. "Think back. What did you really see?"

Through the icy night, I see a black silhouette in the headlights, its large, imposing shadow thrown back over me.

"But the real question is," she says, letting go of my head, which falls with a lifeless thud on the dash, "at this point, what does it matter?"

CHAIN REACTION

The winter sun crept over the crest of Wretched Mountain, spilling down the rocky knoll through the barren birches that lined a half-frozen Miller's Pond. Earnshaw dragged Campbell Slocomb by the boots, split-apart skull oozing little bits of brain, and flipped him over on the steps of the old ranger station. He took his wallet, stuck it in the back of his jeans beside the rusty pair of pliers and flask of whiskey.

Earnshaw jiggled the teeth in his pocket like loose change from a stranger.

He doused body and shack with gasoline, struck a match, stepped back and watched it all burn.

* * *

As Earnshaw sat at the bar last night, he couldn't stop thinking about Amy May. Since her return to Red Willow, just saying her name made him giddy.

"Well, look at what the cat's caught," Campbell said, taking the stool beside him.

Earnshaw now realized the goofy grin plastered across his face. But for once, he didn't care what anybody else thought.

Campbell held up two fingers. "Two Jamesons," he called out. "Looks like I ain't the only one with good news." He dropped the keys to his latest F250 on the counter. Campbell always made a show of picking up the tab.

But tonight wasn't about petty jealousy.

It was about Amy May, who looked as beautiful as when they were kids, sharing hamburgers at Skippy's Drive-In, skimming stones and laughing, the way she could still shoot those little daggers into Earnshaw's heart. He could've sworn she felt it too. Because of the divorce, he knew they had to take things slow. Which had been hard on Earnshaw.

Maybe this was good. He was bursting to tell someone, and who better than Campbell Slocumb, his oldest friend and biggest rival?

"You want to go first?" Campbell said.

"After you," Earnshaw drawled through a cockeyed grin.

"You sure?" said Campbell. "The way you're chewing on that canary I wouldn't want you to choke."

It had started with a second place finish in the 3rd grade science fair, and only got worse the older they got. Sports. Girls. Life. Earnshaw never could compete with Campbell's talent, good looks, or money.

Until now.

"OK," Campbell said, hopping to his feet. "She didn't want me to say anything until the divorce is final—"

Earnshaw's first muddled thought was, How could he possibly know?

"But once the paperwork dries—"

Then that old familiar feeling crept in, and Earnshaw braced for what was coming next.

"Amy May and me are getting married!"

Like a kick to the guts, it was the 3rd grade all over again, all the wires inside snapping, coiling around themselves, choking off the blood supply and making it hard to think.

"Well?" Campbell said. "Ain't you going to say anything?"

"How about we head down to Miller's Pond in the morning? Do a little fishing at the old ranger's station, like we used to when we was kids? To celebrate."

* * *

It was quite simple really, no different than the chemical change that had once earned him that red ribbon in the 3rd grade science fair, a chain reaction that occurs when excessive, pent-up energy is finally released.

Earnshaw had gone back to his place to drink. And he didn't stop. The phone rang all night, but he wasn't giving her the satisfaction of answering it.

Campbell was late picking him up, still dressed in the same clothes as the night before. At first Earnshaw wondered if Campbell was onto him, because he wasn't talking, acting all moody.

After they parked the F250 on the dirt road and began the long hike to Miller's Pond, Earnshaw finally concluded his friend's sullenness was just another example of the rich not appreciating getting richer. Which only pissed off Earnshaw more. Here Campbell'd gotten a girl like Amy May, and he couldn't even be happy about it.

By the time Earnshaw cracked his skull with that rock, he was pretty worked up.

No one in Red Willow ever gave Earnshaw the credit for being as smart as he was. He could've been so much more had he not had the misfortune of living in Campbell Slocumb's mammoth shadow. Like what he was doing here, getting away with murder, a simple but elegant plan. A burnt body only leaves dental records to go on. Which is why Earnshaw had pulled out all Campbell's teeth. He'd extract a few of his own, sprinkle them in the fire, and the authorities would be looking for Campbell for *his* murder.

He'd finally trade places with Campbell Slocumb, once and for good. Fitting. Since he already felt dead inside, and being Earnshaw hadn't earned him a damn thing his whole rotten life.

Earnshaw reached in his back pocket for the whiskey. He was drunk but not quite drunk enough to pull out his own teeth with a pair of rusty pliers. He brought back Campbell's wallet instead. And now he saw the piece of paper sticking out.

Somehow he knew what that flowery handwriting was going to say before he even read a word.

Dear Campbell,

I am sorry but I cannot marry you. Spending this time with Earnshaw again has brought back old feelings. I waited for him once to get up the courage to come to me, and when he didn't, I made the mistake of marrying the wrong man. I can't do that again. You're wonderful, Campbell, and you have so much going for you. But you'll never be Earnshaw.

Love,

Amy May

Earnshaw let the words sink in with the cold winter winds as the hot ashes danced up from the fire. Wretched Mountain never loomed so large. He never thought he'd say it, but he was going to miss this goddamn town.

He balled up the letter and dropped it in the flames, listening to it crackle.

Then he jabbed the pliers into his mouth, clamped on hard to a molar, and pulled with everything he had.

THE CAPTAIN

The Captain's ranch sat atop the highest ridge of Copperhead Canyon. A horseshoe, split-level adobe on a sprawling compound with majestic retired racehorses and a separate servant's quarters spread across soft, manicured greens, juxtaposed against hard red clay and rock. At least, that was my memory of it. Thirty years is a long time.

When I got up there, the stucco house seemed smaller, its exterior water-stained, and several of the terracotta tiles were chipped and in need of replacing. Parking my old Ford in the turn-around, I didn't see any horses, just some broken down tractor gear in burnt, brown fields enclosed by railroad ties that had fallen from the fence. I wasn't any better prepared for what I'd discover inside.

Although it had only been three years since my father's memorial, the Captain's condition had seriously deteriorated. I had erroneously contributed the slight tremors I observed at the service to drinking. The Captain had always been known to enjoy his whiskey.

When his Mexican maid wheeled the Captain in, his expression seemed frozen, like a mask permanently affixed over his real face, a horror movie killer's, and his head lolled to the side. He shook continuously.

"Don't look shocked, boy," he said. "I ain't dead. I have Parkinson's. You know what that is?"

I said I'd heard of it.

"It's a nerve disease. Wires coming from my brain're all fucked up." With a twitchy finger, he tapped his bald skull. "Still the same ol' Captain." He squeezed the arms of his wheelchair. "Put me in this fucking thing about a year ago. You want a drink?" Before I could answer, he barked, "Carmen! Johnny Walker!"

The maid, Carmen, shuffled off.

"You look just your daddy," the Captain said through a pained smile.

My father worked for the Captain back in the '70s. Everyone's father around here did. In those days, the Captain employed half the town. Officially, he helmed a contracting company, patching up roofs, repairing roads, erecting fences. He owned other stuff, too. Like the Eastside bar and grill near the closed down mines on Salt Lick Road, and Marty McGee's, the topless club past the North Highway. Driving in, I'd seen both had closed down.

Carmen brought the bottle and steered the Captain to the long mahogany table in the dining room, a wall of glass overlooking the setting sun to the west. He made a funny face when Carmen brushed his arm as she exited, like he just sucked an extra sour lemon.

Quavering, he reached out with his knuckle and nudged a glass toward me. I cracked the seal and poured.

"Carmen!" he hollered. "Bring me a goddamn straw!"

Carmen shuffled back with a straw, positioning the end between his lips. The Captain sucked down half the glass like he was slurping soda pop. "Fetch the steaks," he ordered. As she walked away, he sneered contemptuously. "I know she's stealing from me." He did not say this to me exactly, just sort of put it out in the air.

The Captain's face flushed red with the alcohol, a warm glow returning to his sallow cheeks. "Tell me, boy, what are your plans now that you're back in town?"

"Find some work, I guess."

"What kind of work?"

"Been on farms most of the last thirty years."

"Ain't no farms around here, boy," he jeered.

Carmen brought the steaks and set them in front of us, two-inch-thick slabs of purple beef in shimmering pools of blood. The Captain's was already cut up into little pieces. No steam rose, their centers cold.

"Just how I like 'em," said the Captain. "Wipe their ass and slice 'em up." He gestured with a juddering fork. "If you can't handle it, I'll have Carmen put yours back on the fire."

I told him it was fine.

There'd never been a Mrs. Captain, not that I knew of. There was his daughter, Sissy, of course, so there must've been one at some point. She and I had gone to school together. Not that she knew who I was. Sissy was a couple years older, lithe and vivacious. Girls like her didn't talk to guys like me.

On the wall behind the Captain, steer horns and wagon wheels hung beside mounted old-time rifles and wild animal heads, artsy paintings of half-naked women in various states of undress.

"You're probably wondering why I asked you here," the Captain said.

I wasn't, really. I'd taken his invitation for a drink at face value. I'd phoned the Captain when I got into town, thinking maybe he could help me get a better deal on a car down in the trailer park.

"I'm sick, boy," he said. "Probably sicker than I look."

I doubted that. He looked pretty sick.

"And I can't do the things I used to do. I need someone to help around the house."

I turned over my shoulder. "What about Carmen?"

"She's a thief. All Mexicans are thieves. And all we got down here are Mexicans. Which means all we got is thieves." With quivering hand, he guided a gob of bloody sinew to his lips, slurping it up like a worm to a fish.

"I don't know," I said, quick to point out I appreciated the offer. "I'm not really good at housekeeping."

"I have a maid for housekeeping," he snapped. "And I have a cook for cooking. Usually. Today's Sunday, so it's just Carmen. What I need is a personal assistant, someone I can trust to handle my...affairs."

"I've been gone a long time."

"I could trust your daddy. I can trust you." He nodded his head toward the back. "You'd have the whole north house to yourself. And I'd pay you a salary." A terse grin forced its way onto thin lips. "You probably remember I'm quite generous when it comes to that sort of thing."

My plan had been to use the money I'd saved over the years to stake a plot in the flats, but I honestly didn't know what I'd do for a job. The Captain had pointed out the obvious; there were no farms in the Canyon. That life was a dead end anyway, which is why I'd come home. I couldn't stomach the thought of scavenging another long, drawn-out winter. I suppose, ultimately, I believed it was fate.

"I won't be happy if you say no," the Captain said, still feigning a smile whose edges threatened to dip.

* * *

Even as a young boy, I'd known there was more to the Captain than met the eye. Maybe it was his larger-than-life personality, a boisterous, behemoth of man towering over a town of slinking deadbeats, or how anytime he visited the trailer park, he'd toss silver dollars to us neighborhood kids, and we'd leap to catch them like they were tiny slivers of shiny dreams. More than likely, though, it was in my mother's face, the way it would drain gray when they found another body floating in the Gila River, how my father would jump a little quicker when the Captain called after that.

And, it would turn out, I wasn't wrong to be concerned. Just wrong what to be concerned about.

It was my third Sunday in, the Captain and I returning from the track. Not a real horse track, which they didn't have in the Canyon, but an off-track betting site, with a hundred TVs, playing races from all over the country. The Captain thought nothing of dropping ten thousand on a single race. He never seemed to come out ahead, or behind, almost always breaking even. I suppose that's the nature of gambling.

We'd taken his town car. The road up the hillside is long, tortuous, and there's a gate with a mounted camera so you could be buzzed in. When we got there, however, the gate was already open. I heard the Captain curse under his breath. I inquired what was wrong but he didn't respond.

At the house, we found a jerry-rigged Monte Carlo in the driveway jacked up on raised tires with polished chrome rims, and a license plate that read "D-Lux."

As I was helping the Captain into his wheelchair, the front door flew open, and a hideously fat woman lumbered down the steps. Had to be close to two hundred and fifty pounds. Humungous. Her massive breasts slung low and flopped bra-less out of a tied-off shirt, and the extra small cut-off jean shorts pinched her thighs into giant red apples. In her fist she clutched a bottle. Behind her, a wire-thin black man, dressed head to toe in a pink terrycloth track-suit, remained on the porch.

When she bent to hug the Captain, he recoiled, and I could smell the toxic fumes emanating from her person three feet away. The obese woman's face was perfectly round, like a moon pie, peppered with purple pockmarks the size of dimes.

I made for his wheelchair to push him inside, but the fat woman bumped me out of the way. "He's *my* father," she said, "I'll do that."

It was only then that I realized it was his daughter, Sissy.

I started after them, but when the Captain hoisted a hand, I took it as a cue that my night was done.

It was a shock to see Sissy like that, since as I say, back in the day she had been such a hot number. I could still picture that dirty blonde blow-dry, like a pin-up Farrah Fawcett wet dream, those classic rock tees clinging tightly to her curves. Sissy had always been on the wild side, toking up in the parking lot, going with college guys over in Scottsdale. What a fall from grace. Her once-famous feather now dimmed field mouse brown, fried like frizzy straw and thinned by alopecia. With the Captain's money, she could've been anything. Instead, she'd chosen to become a crack whore.

That was the talk around the ranch at least. Said she'd been smoking the rock for years, whoring herself to whomever would take her, dealers, derelicts, truckers off the Highway. The Captain had spent tens of thousands on treatment, but to no effect.

Sissy came by the ranch fairly regularly after that, and always with a different sleazy man. High off her rocker, giant moon face cratered with holes where she'd picked herself silly. It was uncomfortable whenever she'd visit. I never knew how much to assert myself. The Captain obviously didn't want her there, yet he simply couldn't say no to her.

I try to give folks the benefit of the doubt, live and let live, but Sissy was utterly irredeemable in my eyes. Every time she came up the ridge, she asked for money. Of course it was never for drugs. It was because the power got turned off, or she needed money to visit the dentist, which was a good one, since Sissy had about seven teeth left. Had it been up to me, I never would've let her inside. But it wasn't up to me.

* * *

I was beneath the kitchen sink, fixing a leaking pipe. Hector, who maintained the grounds, came in for water. A short, stocky man with a bushy mustache and steely grey eyes, he and I often talked. His family remained in Mexico, and he'd wire them money like clockwork. Mexicans are good like that. Worked with a bunch on them on the farms.

Like everyone I spoke with at the ranch, eventually the conversation turned to Sissy.

"Makes you sick, watching what she does to her father," Hector said. "Just waiting on him to die to get the money."

I poked my head from under the sink and asked him to pass me the wrench on the counter. "She is his daughter."

"I suppose," replied Hector, "but she's also a piece of shit drug addict, who's never worked a day in her life, and who has sucked off half the Canyon." Hector shook his head solemnly. "I'm a Christian. I try to see the good in everyone. I've known cold-blooded murderers and convicts of all shades. I can always find something worthwhile, however small. But not her. I used to say God doesn't make mistakes. After dealing with Sissy, I cannot say that anymore."

I laughed a little. It was hard to overlook the irony. Everyone, including Hector, knew how the Captain made his money, loaning it freely, extracting payback ferociously. Hell, he probably imported the very drugs his daughter was hooked on.

"I know, I know," Hector said. "I've heard it all, too. The Captain is a racist, a drug dealer, he's in the mob. But I still work for him. You know why? Because beneath it all beats the big heart of a good man. You read about the new addition to the school?"

"Sure." It had been in the *Gazette* lately, budget cuts threatening programs, forcing busing out of the Canyon, the usual. Until enough hands wrung that the problem was fixed. Or so I thought.

"That was the Captain. Paid for it all. Just like he bailed out the local Boys and Girls Club last month, and donated that new scoreboard at the football field. But you won't see his name anywhere. The Captain has taken care of this town since we were boys and our fathers worked for him. No, he is not a saint. But how many of us are?"

I firmly tightened the nut and crawled out.

Hector handed me a beer.

"When the Captain dies," he said, "Sissy will get it all. And this town, like the rock she burns, will go up in smoke."

As the Captain got weaker, so too the Canyon. More stores closing up, mortgages going under, men being let go at the ranch. During his house calls, I spoke with the doctor, who told me the end was not imminent, that with the Captain's resources he could conceivably live another twenty years. I wasn't so sure.

All the while Sissy only grew fatter, more despicable, and I began to understand what Hector said was true. Sissy was the Captain's weakness. I have never been a judgmental man. A free hand casting the first stone and all that. There was a time when I would've laughed at the suggestion I'd stick my neck out for this town. But after spending so many years drifting, town to town, farm to farm, I knew now we were all tied to the earth of the Canyon. The more time I spent in the Captain's company, the closer I felt to both.

She would not be missed.

* * *

Beyond the North Highway lies a string of single room occupancy hotels, resting spots for transients and hobos, welfare cases, wards of the states, but, primarily, drug addicts like Sissy. Illumined by shrill, loud neon, this strip sizzles pornography, advertising cheap thrills and perversion, concrete and brick bathed a sicker shade of sin.

It had been easy to find where Sissy lived, since so many money orders had been sent care of the Shady Palms Motel. Watching the scene unfold from my truck, I wish I could say I felt any push or pull that what I was about to do was in any way wrong. On stoops, cracked-out hookers and sad-looking johns haggled and groped, while discarded, diseased syringes floated down stream on a bed of piss and vomit. I tried to convince myself a human life meant more than this.

On the farms, I'd been responsible for slaughtering steer, and as a young man, it was not without trepidation. I'd look into pleading eyes, which I swore at times were trying to communicate, begging for my mercy, and when I'd slit their throats and the hot blood would spurt, and the bloated bovine would convulse, spasm, the chains from which they hung clanking and rattling with those final throes, I'd sometimes be moved to tears. But as time passed, I hardened and stopped being influenced by such juvenile emotions. These things did not deserve my pity. They were dumb, thoughtless creatures.

I effortlessly navigated through the slew of junkies and prostitutes, the shamed and fallen who dared not look me in the eye, wedging into Sissy's unlocked room, where I found the great, shapeless thing lying there like a beached whale on her mattress of filth, bulges of blubber poking between cinches of fabric.

I closed the door and turned the lock.

Sissy stirred, a sleepy hand fumbling to untie her top and unleash her gelatinous breasts. "Put the money on the dresser," she slurred, eyelids fluttering. Her eyes opened momentarily. I gazed into them. The dumb, thoughtless creature returned a blank, thoughtless stare.

On the dresser, crumbled-up singles interspersed with condom wrappers, singed Brill-O Pads and half a dozen cheap lighters whose tops had popped from too much heat.

While Sissy began feebly tugging at her tight shorts, I grabbed a pillow from the floor and climbed on top of her round belly that protruded like an engorged, ripe udder. She did not thrash nor convulse nor show half the heart of a steer, instead pawing at my hands like she were lazily swatting a blue bottle fly on a summer afternoon.

A few fleeting moments and it was over.

* * *

Following news of Sissy's death, which had quickly been ruled drug-related, as I knew it would, I expected the Captain to grieve. She was his daughter, after all. Then life at the ranch would slowly return to normal. Without the stress and strain of Sissy, I sincerely believed the Captain's spirits would improve. As deplorable as I found her, I never would've done anything to harm him.

But the Captain never recovered from his grieving. He blamed himself, despite everyone's assuring him he had done all he could. There were no more steak dinners or Johnny Walker conversations. No more trips to bet the horses. And there was no more tending to business, as the men who handled those details came to the house nightly, only to repeatedly be asked to leave. They'd urge me to shake the Captain out of his stupor; to convince him that he had decisions to make, that grieving or not, all of our financial livelihood depended on it. When I'd relay these messages to the Captain, he offered no words, instead lifting a withered, palsied hand to indicate he wished to be left alone.

Then one morning I went to stir the Captain and found him unresponsive. Medics rushed him to the hospital, where he lingered in a coma for three days, and then was gone.

The Captain's fortune had been overestimated, his affairs hardly in order. Banks and vultures descended, soulless scavengers who feast off the carcasses of the dead. They loaded moving vans, auctioned off whatever of value they could find, the steer horns and animal heads and naked ladies.

I packed my bags. I didn't know how much money would be left, or to whom it would go. It didn't concern me any longer. No one remained at the ranch for me to say goodbye.

I piled my belongings into my truck, and slowly navigated the long, narrow pass, descending into the dregs of the flats, which now resembled a ghost town, streets desolate, boarded-up bricks and whitewashed windows.

Bouncing along erupted asphalt on the road out of town, I looked over dry beds of brush and bramble, into the desert sun sinking behind Canyon walls, and turned headlong away from its fading orange light. I made for the North Highway, in search of a new farm before another winter stripped it all bare.

ONE GOOD REASON

"Give me one good reason why I shouldn't shoot you right now," the kid with the gun said.

Christ, Arrington thought, so this is what it's come to? Playing cops and robbers with a greased-up little shit who's watched too many movies.

Maybe this is what you get. After all, Arrington was pushing fifty, a time when a lot of guys would be thinking about hanging it up.

"Come on, hotshot," the kid with the gun said, pressing the 9mm firmly into Arrington's temple. "One good reason."

This was on Cooksey, who could've called and asked what was up, and Arrington would've explained it was a misunderstanding, a shipment got waylaid in customs, and by night's end they'd be getting drunk together somewhere. But that's not the way the game's played these days. Probably wasn't even Cooksey who made the call.

"I asked you a question, mutherfucker," the kid with the gun said, cocking the hammer, his hand unsteady. "Give me one good reason why I shouldn't shoot you right now!"

Arrington was about to tell the little shit with the flipped-up hair to fuck off. He'd been on the wrong end of a gun plenty of times in his life, and one thing he'd learned. Some guys have the stones. And some guys don't. And this little shit, with his fuzzy lip quivering, wasn't shooting anybody.

Then Arrington thought about what was *actually* being asked. One good reason why he, Loomis Arrington, deserved to live.

Goddamn, Arrington thought, that's a good question.

It was the timing of it all that made it bigger than just one man on his knees in an abandoned airport hanger near the Neman's Freeway haggling over a delayed shipment. No, this was a liminal moment, a goddamn crossroads. Judgment Day. It can happen like that sometimes. Call it God. Call it the Universe. But it's a goddamn reckoning.

And the thing was, when Arrington stopped to think about the question, he wasn't feeling so hot about his answer.

He blamed it all on Leonardo da Vinci.

Arrington probably could've circumvented this whole mess had he just picked up the phone and rang Cooksey himself. Problem was he got caught up watching a show on the History Channel at his condo last night about this guy da Vinci, and then it was too late. Arrington had seen pictures of the Mona Lisa and all that, but he never knew just how involved the guy's life was. This da Vinci had his hands in everything, from building cathedrals to debating philosophy. The real kicker was da Vinci's final words.

I have offended God and mankind because my work did not reach the quality it should have.

When Arrington had heard the narrator say that, he just about lost it.

That was some heavy shit. Here was a man who, in addition to being one of the best artists to ever live, was also an architect, a scientist, geologist, and inventor. The guy developed the prototype for the first helicopter, for crissakes. And if a man like *that* wasted his years, what the fuck had Arrington been doing with his?

Arrington had screwed up his marriage. His own son wouldn't talk to him. Fuck, even his dog, Lucky, had recently run away. All the money he'd made, pissed away on the various women who'd come in and out of his life, which was probably why Dolores had up and split. He'd bullied and intimated, cheated, lied, and stolen at will his entire rotten life, all because it was the road most easily traveled.

Now here he was. On his knees in a goddamn airport hanger on some random Wednesday morning, playing twenty questions with one of the Backstreet Boys.

A goddamn reckoning.

"Give me one good reason," the kid said again, "why I shouldn't—"

"I heard you the first time," said Arrington, turning to face the kid. "If you'll shut up, I'll give you the answer." Arrington sniffed hard, sucking in the lingering fumes of a dozen grounded single-engine airplanes. "One good reason, you little shit?" Arrington began to stand. "Because I can do better."

And that was the last thing Loomis Arrington had to say.

Joe Clifford is the author of *Wake the Undertaker* and *Junkie Love*. He lives in the Bay Area. Follow him at www.joeclifford.com

List of Original Publications

"Unpublished Manuscript #36," appeared in *Hobart,* 2007

"Rags to Riches," *Thuglit,* 2010

"Favors," *Dark Sky,* 2009

"The Meat," *Drunken Boat,* 2012

"Red Pistachios," *Thuglit,* 2009

"Copperhead Canyon," *Shotgun Honey,* 2011

"Go," *Darkest before the Dawn,* 2011

"The Exterminator," *Thunderdome,* 2011

"Another Man's Treasure," *Thrillers, Killers 'n' Chillers,* 2011

"Tripping for Biscuits," *Big Bridge,* 2010

The Burn Out," *Thuglit,* 2007

"A Matter of Trust," *A Twist of Noir,* 2011

"A Chain Reaction," *Flash Fiction Offensive,* 2011

"One Good Reason," *Shotgun Honey,* 2011